THE UNDERDOGS

PHILOMEL BOOKS

A division of Penguin Young Readers Group. Published by The Penguin Group.
Penguin Group (USA) Inc., 375 Hudson Street, New York, NY 10014, U.S.A.
Penguin Group (Canada), 90 Eglinton Avenue East, Suite 700, Toronto, Ontario M4P 2Y3,
Canada (a division of Pearson Penguin Canada Inc.). Penguin Books Ltd, 80 Strand, London
WC2R 0RL, England. Penguin Ireland, 25 St. Stephen's Green, Dublin 2, Ireland (a division
of Penguin Books Ltd). Penguin Group (Australia), 250 Camberwell Road, Camberwell,
Victoria 3124, Australia (a division of Pearson Australia Group Pty Ltd). Penguin Books
India Pvt Ltd, 11 Community Centre, Panchsheel Park, New Delhi—110 017, India.
Penguin Group (NZ), 67 Apollo Drive, Rosedale, Auckland 0632, New Zealand (a division
of Pearson New Zealand Ltd). Penguin Books (South Africa) (Pty) Ltd, 24 Sturdee Avenue,
Rosebank, Johannesburg 2196, South Africa. Penguin Books Ltd, Registered Offices:
80 Strand, London WC2R 0RL, England.

Published simultaneously in Canada. Printed in the United States of America.
Edited by Michael Green. Designed by Amy Wu. Text set in 12-point Oranda BT.

Library of Congress Cataloging-in-Publication Data
Lupica, Mike. The Underdogs / Mike Lupica. p. cm.
Summary: Small but fast twelve-year-old Will Tyler, an avid football player
in the down-and-out town of Forbes, Pennsylvania, takes matters into his own hands to try
and finance the city's football team, giving the whole community hope in the process.
[1. Football—Fiction. 2. Community life—Pennsylvania—Fiction.
3. Pennsylvania—Fiction.] I. Title. PZ7.L97914Un 2011 [Fic]—dc23 2011011762

ISBN 978-0-399-25001-9
1 3 5 7 9 10 8 6 4 2

THE UNDERDOGS

MIKE LUPICA

Philomel Books / An Imprint of Penguin Group (USA) Inc.

For my pal Elmore Leonard

ACKNOWLEDGMENTS

As always, my wife Taylor and my four children—
Christopher, Alex, Zach, Hannah—
inspire me every single day.

But I also want to give special thanks
on this book to four others:
Gerry Callahan, who shared so much
of his passion for youth football.
The great Esther Newberg, who imagined
this group of underdogs even before I did.
And my Mom and Dad.
Just because.

01

Just about everybody who'd ever seen Will Tyler play said the same thing—that he could fly on a football field.

He was definitely flying now.

Ball tucked firmly in the bend of his arm, open field in front of him. A slight wind at his back. Not that he needed it.

At midfield he made an effortless cut to his left, switching the ball from his right hand to his left in the process.

Will did it without even thinking, did it on instinct, one more move that nobody had to teach him. Not even his dad, who'd been a star running back in this same town, on this same field.

Back when the field was in much better shape. And the town was, too.

But Will's dad always said that even on his best days, all the way through high school, he was never as fast as Will.

"You've got that gear," he told Will once.

"What gear?"

"That extra gear that the great ones have," Joe Tyler said.

Will shifted into that gear now.

Flying, like the wind at Shea Field wasn't just behind him, it was trying to keep *up* with him.

At the thirty he cut back again, back to his right, angling toward the sideline. Switching the ball back to his right hand. Imagining that he was watching himself on one of those giant screens most NFL stadiums have now, pretending he was trying to see if anybody was gaining on him.

Knowing that nobody would be.

Twenty-yard line now.

Fifteen.

Only the end zone ahead of him.

And that's when he went down.

He hadn't been tackled. He'd stepped into a hole at the five-yard line.

He hadn't seen it because he had his eye on the prize, like always. Just felt his right foot go into it, the leg collapsing, like he'd been tripped. Like he'd been caught from behind. Just like that.

Will was mad. The beat-up field at Shea was the only thing that could stop him. And it had. And had cost him a touchdown. Of course he knew it could have been worse, he could have rolled an ankle or hurt his knee the way his dad had once. It had been his senior year in high school. His dad hadn't stepped into a hole, though. He'd just made a cut into the secondary and thought he was about to break into the clear when he got hit by tacklers from both sides, at the same exact moment, their helmets meeting at his right knee.

In so many ways, too many ways for Will to even count, it was a hit from which his dad still hadn't recovered.

Will had gone down hard but knew he was all right, knew he would have no trouble getting back up. The only burn he was feeling now was embarrassment.

The same he'd felt last season after the fumble against Castle Rock.

He sat there, ball under his arm, thinking:

It's a good thing I'm alone.

Alone with his ball, alone on this field, no teammates or opponents there to see him trip and go down, nobody to see somebody this good at football look so bad.

He turned and saw how deep the hole was. One of many at Shea Field, a field that the town seemed to have forgotten, or maybe just given up on, the way it was about to give up on a football team and a football season for twelve-year-olds like Will Tyler.

The town council of Forbes had made it clear a couple of weeks earlier that there wasn't enough money in the budget to finance all the local sports teams, as it had in the past. They'd said that some of the younger age groups might have to suffer so that no programs were cut at Forbes High School. They'd said it was more expensive than ever to finance football teams, telling the parents there had been barely enough in the budget to let Will's eleven-year-old team compete last season in the West River Youth Football League, Forbes's version of Pop Warner. Now unless somebody in town could come up with the money in a few weeks, enough money to cover membership in the league, helmets, uniforms, field maintenance, emergency services, insurance—what Will's dad called "the full boat"—there would be no football for twelve-year-olds this year.

No team, no practices, no games, no shot at the league title Forbes had come within a touchdown of winning last season.

Maybe, Will thought—alone on this field, two yards short of the end zone—a run like this in an imaginary game would be the only kind he would get to make this year.

02

Will felt as if football was about to leave Forbes the way the sneaker factory had.

Technically the factory hadn't left, he knew. It was still there on the river, only it was empty now the way it had been for most of Will's life. It was the business that had left, the business that used to make Forbes Flyers, once one of the most famous athletic-shoe brands in the country.

That was before other companies began to dominate the business with cool sneakers of every color, for every sport. And even cooler catchphrases and commercials, with endorsements from the hottest athletes. Those other companies became what his dad called the "superpowers" of the sneaker business, and they had wiped out Forbes Flyers like powerful armies invading a tiny nation.

"It wasn't that Nike or any other others were doing anything wrong," Joe Tyler told Will once. "They were just selling shoes and giving the people what they wanted. But in the process, it was like they wiped out the world we'd grown up in, the one built around that factory."

Now his dad wondered how Forbes Flyers had held on as long as they had, before the shoes with the cool wings logo finally just disappeared.

When they did, the factory where his father had worked and his grandfather before him went with them. Some of the people who had worked there found other jobs in Forbes. A lot more moved away.

Will knew all about it by now, the sad history of the business and the town, just because he'd grown up hearing his dad talk about it so much, like somehow his own life story was tied up with the story of the Forbes Flyers. It was like a book Will had not just read, but re-read, a movie he had seen over and over again. Families gone. Friends gone. Houses empty and yards ignored. Will was pretty sure that the only successful business in Forbes was the one that printed the "For Sale" signs.

And yet across the river sat the town of Castle Rock, home of Castle Rock Springs, the bottled water company that was thriving. It was only a few miles from Forbes to Castle Rock. To Will it felt like the people who lived there, the kids growing up there, were on the other side of the world. A world people moved *to* and not away *from*. A world where people didn't worry about abandoned neighborhoods and empty factories and football seasons lost.

Guys Will's age were going to have a season over there, that was for sure. Another great season, no doubt. The kind they always seemed to have, playing on a two-year-old turf field that was in better condition than most of the high school fields in the area. Wearing the new uniforms they got every single year.

There were a lot of days when Will would sit by himself on the river and just stare at the world across the water, wanting to be over there, wanting to play on their team. He never said that out loud to anybody, certainly not to his dad. He would never say anything in front of his dad that sounded like whining or complaining, no way. Not when he knew the story of his dad's life, knew how hard he had worked to take care of Will from the time his mom had died, back when Will was just two years old.

How hard his dad was still working.

It didn't change the fact that Will thought he was growing up on the wrong side of the river.

At dinner that night Will said to his dad, "How come we can't play one more season with last year's uniforms? That would save us some money right there."

His dad started to smile, then stopped himself, as if he knew none of this was funny to Will.

"Last season *was* the one more season with those uniforms," his dad said. "After the last game, they bagged them up and carted them away. Helmets, pads, the whole deal."

"Then we're going to have to raise the money ourselves," Will said.

"Who's *we*?" his dad said.

"The guys on the team."

"All fourteen of you?"

There were times last season when only eleven guys suited up for games. It was as if some of the kids—or their parents—were giving up on football before football gave up on them.

Will said, "We can do it."

"In two weeks?"

Will managed a smile. "Hey, whose side are you on?"

"Yours," his dad said. "Always. But you've got about as much chance of finding that money in Forbes right now as you have of finding gold in the river."

His dad had gotten home late tonight. He was still wearing the shorts he wore in summer when he was delivering the mail.

Will pounded the table, hard enough that his water glass started to tip over before he caught it.

"I'm not letting them take football away from me!" he said. "They're not supposed to be able to do that."

In a quiet voice his dad said, "And the factory wasn't supposed to shut down. And the banks weren't supposed to own half the houses in town."

"But, Dad," Will said, "I can ..."

He didn't need to finish the thought, because his dad did it for him.

"You can flat-out *play*," Joe Tyler said. "Nobody knows that better than I do. Now that's enough complaining. Finish your dinner."

Will *could* play. He wasn't the biggest kid his age in Forbes, or even close. Truth was, he was closer to being the smallest in his seventh-grade class, height-wise, than he was to being the biggest. When he'd shown up for tryouts last season, the coach thought Will was too small to be a halfback.

That lasted until they were midway through their first scrimmage, Will finally getting his chance to line up behind the quarterback. He took a handoff on what was supposed to be a simple belly play and turned it into an eighty-yard run.

That was when Coach Jerry York, found out that Will could fly.

By the time the regular season was over, he'd scored sixteen touchdowns in eight games and Forbes, even though there were those days when they only suited up the mandatory eleven and prayed nobody would get hurt, made it all the way to the West River championship game before losing to Castle Rock.

Will scored three touchdowns that day and gained nearly two hundred rushing yards. All before the hit from behind caused him to fumble the ball at the Castle Rock ten-yard line with only sixteen seconds left to play.

Will felt terrible, as if he'd let his entire team down. He still felt terrible about that fumble. But when the game was over, the Castle Rock quarterback, Ben Clark, whose father owned the bottled-water company, grabbed Will and said, "The only thing you did wrong today was wear the wrong uniform. Dude, next season you gotta come play with us."

Will thanked him but said he was fine where he was. Thinking that the only thing he wanted to do next season was come back and beat those guys, straight up.

Only now there might not be a next season.

"It's not fair," he said to his dad now, knowing that he was right up against that line, the poor-me line he couldn't cross.

"You're right," Joe Tyler said, taking his plate over to the sink. "It's not fair. Soon as we clean up, I'll add it to the list of the other things in life that aren't."

Will could see how tired his dad was, knew it had been one of those days when he was off the truck and delivering mail in town on foot.

On that knee.

It was one of the reasons Will worked so hard not to complain—not to cross that line—because his dad almost never did, even though he had a lot more reason to.

There was a long silence between them while they did the dishes, his dad washing and Will drying, Will wanting to change the subject from his own problems with the team. So he finally said, "How was work?" because that was the best he could do.

His dad said, "Sometimes I think they'll close down the Postal Service the way they did the sneaker factory. There won't be paper mail anymore, just e-mail. Don't need a postman for e-mail."

Then he walked slowly up the stairs, limping slightly, to take a hot shower, saying he'd be back later to watch the Steelers preseason game.

Once, Will knew, his dad had dreamed about going to Pitt to play college football, or Penn State, or even Notre Dame. Back when he was the star running back in town.

That was before his knee exploded.

He said he still loved football, but Will wasn't so sure, wasn't sure if watching the games was another kind of hurt for Joe Tyler. But he said he loved the Steelers as much as he ever had and would make a show of getting into the games, even though on nights like this, Will knew his dad's enthusiasm for the game would fade. That there would be a time in the second half when he'd look over and his dad's chin would be on his chest and he would be snoring softly.

It was still early in tonight's game, midway through the first quarter, when Will's dad surprised him, as though Joe Tyler had been having a conversation inside his own head and was only now deciding to include Will.

"We can't move," he said.

Meaning, to Castle Rock.

"Dad, I know that. I'm not an idiot."

"I'm not working in another factory. Did it once. Once was enough."

It was another story Will knew by heart, how his dad, along with half the population in Forbes, had been laid off when the Forbes Flyers doors shut for good.

All those jobs, just gone.

Will knew a lot about his dad. Like how he had grown up with Ben Clark's and Toby Keenan's dads here in Forbes, how the three of them had played high school football together until Joe Tyler hurt his knee. How they'd all grown apart after that. How many years later Mr. Clark had started over with the bottled-water plant in Castle Rock and had offered Joe Tyler a chance to work there, telling him he could start on the assembly line with an eye toward moving up to a management position.

How Will's dad turned him down. Just like Will had turned Ben down.

To Joe Tyler a factory was a factory. Being trapped inside one symbolized everything that had gone wrong in his life since he'd hurt his knee.

Now Will said, "Dad, I'd never ask you to take a job you hate."

"Sometimes," his dad said, not looking at Will, "I drive by in the mail truck and see you sitting on the riverbank."

"I like looking at the water, you know that. I always have."

"You're my dreamer, pal. You think I don't know some of your dreams?"

Will smiled. His dad must have felt it on him, because he turned now and smiled back.

Joe Tyler said, "It's my own fault, the way I've turned out."

"You've turned out great," Will said, knowing the words came out too fast.

"Hush and listen. The only job I ever really cared about was football. I never saw myself as anything other than a football player." The smile was gone now, just like that. "I won't let you make the same mistake I did, putting all your eggs in one stupid basket."

Will didn't want to have this conversation tonight, one they'd had before. The one about there being more to life than football.

Not when you're twelve, Will thought. *And not when they're about to take your season away.*

Right before halftime, Will heard the snoring next to him. He got up, lowered the volume on the TV, went upstairs and fired up his old Dell laptop, the one the guy at the little computer repair store downtown was already calling "vintage."

Will went to Google and looked up *Forbes Flyers* the way he had many times before and stared at the pictures of the cool old high-top black football shoes with the wings on the sides. It was a way to take himself back to when his town was still a real town, when flying still seemed possible.

But he couldn't help himself and began to look at this year's shoes, a pair of New Balance 897 cleats, for grass fields, and the 996 turf shoe, for turf fields like the one Castle Rock had. Both reminded him of the old Forbes Flyers.

Will Tyler looked at a pair of football shoes he might never get to wear for a long time, like he was shopping for an iPhone he might never own, or an iPad.

He powered down the Dell thinking, *What's the point?*

That's when the idea hit him.

One Hail Mary pass to save the season.

03

I t was the end of August. The unofficial end of summer.
Usually Will couldn't wait for school to start.

It wasn't for the classroom part or the studying part. Certainly not for the homework part. Will was an average student, at best. He looked forward to school for one reason only: the start of football.

And he wasn't alone, even though the number of kids his age trying out for football in Forbes seemed to get smaller every year, the way the town did.

"The way I see it," Tim LeBlanc said to Will the next morning at Shea, "we might as well skip school this year. Or at least the hard parts."

"All due respect," Will said, "but what parts of school aren't hard for you?"

Tim said, "You ever notice how nothing good ever comes after 'all due respect'? It's like asking your punter to make a tackle.

What comes after it hurts no matter how you look at it. Kind of like this plan of yours. All due respect and all."

Will had told Tim about his Hail Mary play first thing when they got to Shea. But Tim had reacted as if Will had told him he was putting an SOS note in a bottle and setting it adrift at sea.

Will wasn't discouraged.

A good play was a good play.

Tim had been Will's blocking back from the time they'd started playing on the team for ten-year-olds. He was a head taller than Will and outweighed him by at least twenty pounds, and if the offensive line didn't open up the holes for him, Tim did. Tim's weight, in fact, was one of the reasons that Forbes had quit the Pop Warner league two years ago and helped form the West River league.

When they were in fifth grade, Tim had barely made it under the weight limit for guys their age. After the season was done, Tim's dad said that he wasn't going to make his kid lose five pounds, or whatever it was, the next season if he wanted to keep playing football.

"I'm against kids being told they're *too* anything," Nick LeBlanc had said at the time. "Too big, too small, too slow, too anything."

The crazy thing, at least to Will, was that Mr. LeBlanc was now the president of the town council. Meaning he was now one of the adults telling Will and Tim that their town was too poor to play in their league this season.

Tim loved playing football almost as much as Will did, just for the sheer fun of knocking people over on offense and defense. Yet he acted like it was his job now—maybe because his dad was coming across as one of the bad guys—to explain what he called "the dollars" to his best bud.

He started explaining them again to Will now.

"You make the money we need sound like a million dollars," Will said. "It's not."

"No," Tim said. "But the ten thousand might as *well* be a million right now."

Ten thousand dollars. Tim had already explained to Will what the money bought:

The equipment, first of all. The cost of the vans needed to transport kids to the away games. The fee for someone, a firefighter or police officer or nurse, to handle the EMT van at games in case somebody got hurt. Money to pay officials for home games. And an insurance fee.

Will imagined the numbers stacking up against him like guys on the other side of the football trying to stop him on a short-yardage play.

Ten. Thousand. Dollars.

Just the cost of new uniforms alone was going to be about five hundred dollars per player. Most of that went for new helmets, in a world where grown-ups kept trying to make the helmets safer every single year because of all the attention being paid to concussions, from boy leagues all the way up to the pros.

Especially in the boy leagues.

Will and Tim took a break from throwing passes to each other, sitting in the grass in one end zone, the day stretching out in front of them the way summer days were supposed to. Even late-summer days. Nowhere to be right now except here.

"Well, I woke up feeling lousy about our situation," Tim said, "but now I show up here and find out that my man is a man with a plan. And, as everybody knows, where there's a Will . . ."

Why did everybody think that joke was so stinking funny?

"Don't," Will said. "I mean it."

"Touchy."

"About this? *Yeah.*"

The last word came out in two parts, as if Will had broken it in half.

Tim said, "Thrill, you know I always believe you can do things nobody else can."

Tim had nicknamed him Will the Thrill, or just Thrill, explaining that every time Will had the ball in his hands, there was a decent chance he would be taking it to the house.

"But you gotta know," Tim said, "that stuff like this only works in the movies."

"You don't know that."

"I have a lot of opinions on things I don't know about."

Will said, "Tell me about it."

"Hey, just because I'm an idiot doesn't mean I'm always wrong."

Will was on his back, throwing the ball into the air, thinking how great it looked against the blue sky, catching it.

"I even thought about writing to Mr. Castle Rock."

It's what they called Ben Clark's dad.

"Come on, man!" Tim said, sounding like one of the guys on ESPN. "That would be like the Steelers going to the Ravens and asking for help."

"I know," Will said. "It's why I didn't do it. We can't take a handout from them and then go try to beat them."

Will gripped the ball, stood up, said, "Go deep."

"I was born to catch passes."

"No, you were born to open holes for me."

"Tragically, the only holes we might have to worry about this season are the ones in the ground here."

Tim took off down the field. Will yelled after him, "You gotta believe!"

Over his shoulder Tim yelled, "I know you stole that from some old guy."

Will let the ball go, a perfect spiral, not bad for a running back. Just as Tim reached for it, *he* stepped in one of the holes in the field and went down the way Will had the day before.

It was hard to get Will to laugh these days.

But he laughed now.

At noon Will and Tim went their separate ways, knowing they'd be back by two o'clock, when a bunch of the guys from last year's team would be gathering for a game of touch football.

Before he left, Tim said, "You gonna tell the other guys your plan?"

"I wouldn't call it a plan, exactly. More like what it is. A prayer."

"But are you gonna tell?"

"Not yet. I don't want them to get their hopes up."

"But it's okay to do that with me?"

"Look at it this way," Will said. "This time I'm the one trying to open the hole. One big enough for a whole team to run through."

Will walked home to have lunch by himself. It was that way for him most of the time. Sometimes, Will's dad would meet him at home for a quick sandwich before heading back to work.

Other times, even if he was walking the downtown route, he'd hustle home to do the same thing, Will watching him eat with one hand and rub his bad knee with the other.

But today, Will knew, his dad was on the other side of Forbes. So the house was absolutely quiet. It was a quiet he'd grown used to, a part of his life from the time he'd been old enough to be in the house alone. Even then his dad would make sure that one of the neighbors would be home, either Mrs. Pomerantz on one side or Mrs. Bailey on the other.

It was the kind of quiet that only having a mom could change.

He had no memory of Ellen Tyler. Just pictures. And old home movies he'd never watched. But the pictures were everywhere in the house, showing a pretty, dark-haired woman smiling at the camera, Will almost always in her arms or at her side.

In one of them, she had her arms out, laughing, as Will came to her. Will's dad told him it was taken when he was first learning to walk.

Someday, he told himself, he'd watch the movies.

Just not yet.

One time Tim had been talking, not really thinking about what he was saying, and he told Will that he couldn't remember a single time in his life when he walked through the front door of his house after school, or at lunchtime in the summer, and his mom wasn't there waiting for him.

As soon as he'd said it, he knew.

"Oh, man, I'm sorry," Tim had said.

"No worries."

"You can't be dumber than me."

"Well," Will had said, forcing a smile, "we sort of knew that already. Seriously, dude, forget it."

Only Will never had. Ever since, he'd think about those words whenever he came into the small two-story house on Valley Road. Not the one his mom and dad had lived in when they had first gotten married, over on the other side of town, closer to the factory. His dad had sold that one the month after the funeral, and he and Will had lived in an apartment for a couple of years before they moved to the house on Valley.

The only time Joe Tyler went past his old house near the factory was when he was delivering mail. He'd never even taken Will to see it.

"That was one life, bud. Now you and me got another one going, just the two of us."

Then his dad used a football expression he used a lot. "The ball's not round," he said. "It'll take some funny bounces on you. You still gotta pick it up and keep running."

Will checked his e-mail first thing when he got to the house, knowing it was ridiculous to think he might have already gotten a reply. Or that he'd *ever* get a reply. He wasn't even going to tell Tim he'd checked when they met up back at Shea for the touch football game.

That didn't mean he was giving up hope.

He made himself a peanut butter sandwich, washed it down with a glass of milk. Went back upstairs, checked his e-mail again. Nothing. Came back down, watched a little bit of SportsCenter, saw a couple of reports from the pro-football training camps. Grabbed a Gatorade to take with him back to the field, knowing he was going to get there before anybody else. He didn't care. Even now, he was happier at Shea than anywhere else. It was a football field. In Will's mind, even a bad field was better than none. And there was going to be a game today, even if it was touch, even if it wound up four-on-four or five-on-five.

As far as Will was concerned, whatever the numbers, he would be happy to play, even if it was just until dinnertime. When he and the guys would get together like this, it was a day he never wanted to end.

About a block from Shea, Will started to run, Gatorade in his left hand, football in his right. He ran easily at first, then picked up the pace, finally going full tilt, cutting around the hedges that enclosed one end of the field.

He had just made his turn toward the field when a ball came out of the air and hit him on the head.

That's when he looked up and saw the girl.

04

He was lucky it didn't catch him square in the face instead of the side of his head, right above his ear. It still rang his bell.

Big-time.

Will looked down at the ball and saw that it was the same as the one his dad had bought him last Christmas, a regulation NFL ball, with the commissioner's signature under the laces.

He reached down and felt it, understanding why the inside of his head was buzzing: the sucker was as hard as a rock.

Will took another look in the direction where it had come from and saw that the girl was the only person at Shea. She was standing about forty yards away, right in the middle of the field. She looked to be a little taller than Will was, or maybe a lot, with long hair, long legs. When she saw him staring at her, she put a hand up, as if to say "my bad."

No kidding, Will thought.

He carried both balls toward her, along with the Gatorade bottle he'd managed not to drop. When he was close enough to her, this girl he'd never seen before, she said, "I yelled for you to look out, but you must not have heard me."

Will said, "Yell louder next time. And I'm okay, by the way. Thanks for asking."

"C'mon," she said, "how bad could it have been? You didn't even go down." Smiling now. "Like you did yesterday when the ground tripped you up." She snapped her fingers and said, "And so close to pay dirt."

"Wait a second. You were *here*? Watching me?"

"Not spying on you, if that's what you're suggesting. Just waiting for you to clear the field after your game of one-on-*none*. Do you cut back that well when there are actual players on the field?"

He couldn't help it, he felt embarrassed now, worried that his face might be getting red. Picturing himself zigzagging down the field like a maniac and then ending up on the ground. Knowing something, even at the age of twelve: no guy wants to look clumsy or weird in front of a girl, even one he doesn't know.

He was about to ask for her name when she said, "I was just trying to see if I could kick one over the hedges. But I was wide right." She smiled again. "As you found out, the hard way."

"Hold on," Will said.

He turned and took a good look at where the hedges were on Arch Street, near the arches that were the entrance to Shea.

"You," Will said, "kicked a football, *this* football, from here to *there?"*

She shrugged. "Usually I'm a lot more accurate."

"No way."

"I'm just putting this out there," she said. "But *way."*

"Punt or placekick?"

"Seriously? Placekick. If I'd punted it, you would have just seen it flying overhead, like an airplane."

"You can't kick it that far."

"And you know this . . . how?"

"Nobody I know who's my age . . . How old are you?"

"Twelve."

"No twelve-year-old in town can kick a ball that far." Now Will looked around at her feet. "Where's the tee, then?"

She smiled again. As annoying as she was, Will had to admit it was a pretty great smile. "Now you're just being plain old mean. A *tee?"* Still smiling at him, she said, "Tees are, like, for *boys."*

"Funny."

"I have my moments. But what's *really* funny is that you seem to be telling me that since no twelve-year-old boy you know could kick one that far, it would be impossible for a girl to do it."

"I'm just saying."

"Saying *that."*

"Yeah," Will said. "I guess I am."

"Well, at least we're clear on one thing."

"What?"

"Getting bonked on the head didn't knock any sense into you."

Will shook his head. "I think I got it now. Before long, I'll be apologizing to you because I got hit by a ball you *say* you kicked that far."

"If I didn't," she said, "how'd the ball get there?"

Will had no answer for that one, so he said, "Do it again."

"Fine with me," she said. "Your ball or mine?"

"Your call."

"Yours."

Will handed her his ball, which looked a lot older, a lot more worn than hers. Hers had that shiny feel you got with one just out of the box.

"You want me to be your holder?"

She said, "No, thank you."

He noticed she was wearing khaki-colored shorts with big pockets on them that came to her knees, old Converse sneakers with no laces, and a black Manchester United T-shirt. A pretty cool shirt, Will thought.

She placed the ball gently in a patch of grass that was a little higher than what was around it, getting it to stand up on its own. Placing the ball like she knew what she was doing.

When it was just right, she said, "There." Not to Will. Merely pleased with herself that the ball was the way she liked it, tilted just slightly toward her. Already Will had the feeling that this girl was pleased with herself a *lot*.

Then she turned and measured off her paces, stopped and took two steps to her left, the way placekickers did in real games.

Ready now.

Well, almost.

First, she smiled again at Will, her biggest one yet, like she was giving him the full force of her. "Sure you don't want to call your last time-out and freeze me?" she said.

"Sure you don't want to put off throwing up a brick a little longer?"

"I'm good."

She took a deep breath, blew it out hard, made her move at the ball on her long legs, planted her left foot, and swung her right leg through, soccer style, like a champ.

In the quiet of Shea field, the sound of her foot hitting the ball was like a door slamming.

They both watched the ball sail through the air, end over end, until it cleared the hedges with ease and disappeared onto Arch Street.

She had buried it.

She closed her fist and pumped her arm.

"*Yes!*"

Then she came over to Will and extended a hand to him.

"Hannah Grayson," she said. "*Now* you know somebody in town who can kick it that far."

05

Until now, Will thought he knew every seventh grader in Forbes, especially since the only private school in town, St. Cecilia's, had been forced to close—not enough money to keep *it* open, either—and all kids his age went to Forbes Middle School.

Not only had he never met this girl, he wasn't sure he'd ever met a girl *like* her.

She had been talking smack to him from the moment he'd shown up, chirping him, as Tim liked to say, and now she was trying to convince him to retrieve a ball she'd kicked into the street.

"You have to get it," she said.

"Why is that? You kicked it."

"Kicked it farther than you thought I could. Right there is the reason why you should go get it."

She had a point, but Will wasn't about to give ground. Mostly because he felt as if he'd been doing that since her first kick had caught him upside the head. He said, "Nope. You kicked it, you fetch it."

Hannah said, "Look at it another way. If we'd been shooting hoops, and I'd made a shot from the outside, who rebounds?"

Will sighed. "I do."

Hannah didn't say anything, just put her hands out like she was resting her case.

"Okay, I give up," Will said. He ran and got the ball where it was sitting in the middle of Arch Street and brought it back.

"Where'd you come from?" he said.

"Today?" she said. "Or in general?"

"If you lived here, I'd know you. So you either just moved here or you're just visiting."

"Just moved here."

"I didn't think anybody moved *to* Forbes anymore," he said. "Just *away*."

"That's what my mom keeps saying to my dad. But he works for the company that owns a bunch of small newspapers in western Pennsylvania and eastern Ohio. So they sent him here to find out if the *Dispatch* is worth saving or if they should put it out of its misery."

"Like Forbes?"

Hannah said, "You said it, not me."

The Forbes *Dispatch*, which still landed on Will's front porch every morning, was the only paper in town, and even with that, it seemed to be getting thinner and thinner all the time. Will's dad had been predicting for the last year or so that before long, it would be just one more business in Forbes to go under, and everybody in town would get their news from the Internet.

"Does your dad think he can save it?"

Hannah said, "You don't know my dad, but he thinks if somebody put him in charge of the Pirates, he could get *them* turned around. He's a little cocky that way."

"There's a stunner."

She looked at him, hands on hips, trying to look offended, not selling it very well as far as Will could tell. "You're saying I'm cocky?"

"Only if I could dial you down a little."

She frowned, like she was trying to do a math problem in her head, Will figuring she was trying to think up a good comeback. But finally she surprised him and just said, "Good one."

"So you're going into seventh?"

"Yes sir."

"You play sports?"

"I played soccer in Toledo. Center middie. Our team went unbeaten and won the states. But my dad says there might not even be a girls team this year in Forbes."

"Or boys. And not just in soccer."

"Yeah," she said. "That must be a chafe for you."

"More than a chafe. One thing you could always say about growing up here is that you were growing up in football country.

All of a sudden it's like some kind of foreign country, at least on this side of the river."

"What are you going to do if there's no season? Go play in Castle Rock? That's what I might do in soccer."

"I can't."

"Why not?"

"It's a long story," he said.

Like the Hail Mary pass was. But he wasn't going to share that with her. It would be just another way for her to make fun of him.

"Why didn't you guys move to Castle Rock?" Will asked.

"My dad," she said. "He said that if he was going to publish the Forbes newspaper, he was going to *live* in Forbes. Game, set, match."

Without either one of them saying anything, they sat down in the grass at the same time. Will offered her some Gatorade, but she'd brought her own. He asked where she lived and she said on Arch Street, not giving him the address.

Will said, "I gotta admit: you *do* kick better than any guy I know."

"I can do most things better than most guys you know," she said. "Like throw and catch. And hit a baseball. I'd say run faster, too, except after watching you play your little fantasy ball the other day, I'm not sure I could beat you in a running race."

"Wow," Will said. "A compliment directed at somebody besides yourself?"

"My dad says if you can do something, it's not bragging."

Will said, "My dad says that when you get to the end zone, you're supposed to act as if you've been there before."

She laughed. "Well," she said, "at least that wasn't an issue when I was watching you do your belly flop yesterday."

"It may have been a flop, but if you were watching, you noticed I landed on another part of my body."

"I'm surprised you couldn't hear me laughing."

"I fell in a hole!"

"Keep telling yourself that."

"Have you met any other kids since you moved?" Will said. "Or am I the first friend you're *not* making?"

"Ooh," she said, "Willie gets off another good one."

"None of my friends calls me Willie. Ever."

"Who said we were going to be friends?"

"Are you always this tough?"

"How come when girls give it back, they're tough? And guys are just being guys?"

"I give up," he said.

He looked over her shoulder then, toward the hedges, and saw Tim and Jeremiah Keating, who would have been their team's best wideout this season, coming around from Arch Street.

"Hey," Will said, "we're gonna have a game of touch in a few. You can hang around and play if you want."

Then he added: "Show my friends how much better you are than them."

"Maybe another time," she said. "I've got somewhere I need to be."

Will couldn't help it. "You're not scared, are you?" he said.

"Yeah," she said. "Scared of the competition here in Nowhere, Pennsylvania."

She grabbed her ball and her Gatorade bottle. Stood up and over Will for a second. Then she started jogging down the field, toward the end zone where Will had fallen.

There was a part of Will, a *big* part, hoping she would do the same.

She didn't. She had the ball in her right hand and when she got to the fading chalk line of the thirty-yard line, she stopped suddenly, planted like a quarterback who'd just avoided a rush, squared her shoulders, and fired a perfect spiral high in the air, as high as her kick had been.

Splitting the uprights with the pass.

This time Hannah Grayson chased down her own ball, picked it up and disappeared down the winding path that took you back to Arch Street. Gone, without looking back.

By then Tim and Jeremiah were standing with Will.

"Who was *that*?" Jeremiah said.

Will exhaled. Loudly. Not quite sure where to start.

"Boys," he said finally, "*that* was a girl."

06

They played all afternoon.

They'd finish a game and switch the teams around and then start another game. Five-on-five. Bobby Carrington, the team's quarterback last season, hadn't shown up, so everyone took turns playing quarterback.

Now it was the last game of the day, since it was getting close to dinnertime. Only, the game wouldn't end, so they finally came up with a variation of the overtime format used in college football.

One team got the ball at midfield and if they scored, the other team had to score for them to keep playing. If the first team didn't score, the other team could win with a touchdown.

After two rounds of overtime—no more first downs. Score in four plays or turn over the ball.

Both teams kept scoring anyway.

And even though it was just a touch football game with a

bunch of buds, even though most guys were dragging at the end, even though they all had dinner waiting for them, here was the thing: *nobody would settle for a tie.*

Chris Aiello, the biggest guy on the field, said, "I'd rather lose than tie."

"Same," Tim said.

They were in their huddle. Will shook his head, grinning at them. "You know today's result doesn't count in the standings, right? It's not going to affect our playoff position?"

Chris said, "Are we keeping score today?"

"Well, obviously," Will said.

"Then it counts. Now call a play so we can end this. I'm hungry."

Tim said, "When aren't you?"

They'd finally stopped Jeremiah's team in what felt like the ninth overtime, but only because Jeremiah had dropped a wide-open pass in the end zone, not because anybody on defense had any legs left. So if Will's team scored, the game would be over.

Will said he'd play QB. He gave them all their pass patterns, then took the snap from Chris. Jeremiah, totally gassed now, was left to rush the passer. He loudly counted out until he got to five-Mississippi and then came after Will.

Will gave one last look down the field and smiled to himself.

Then he took off past Jeremiah. As soon as he did, he heard somebody from the defense yell out, "He's running!"

Will ran, taking it up the middle of the field at first. He'd sent

Chris and Tim deep and now saw the guys who'd been covering them, Wes Blabey and Brandon Spikes, running toward him from both sidelines.

They did have the angle on him and probably thought they could keep him in the middle of the field, where they could converge on him.

But when they had almost reached him, Will put one of his best moves on him. He wasn't quite at full speed—not yet—so he was able to plant a foot and spin, turning his back on Wes and Brandon, giving them what he called his 180, and just like that he was on his way to the right sideline.

Leaving them in his dust.

Will heard one of them say, "Get out of here."

That's exactly what I'm doing, Will thought, running down the sideline.

He gave one last look behind him, over his left shoulder, legs pumping, hearing his own breath, and saw that Jeremiah was still chasing the play.

He might as well have been chasing a car.

Will switched into that extra gear, just for the fun of it. He ran straight through the end zone, not doing anything fancy with the ball, no dopey dance steps. No showboating. It wasn't his style.

Act like you've been there before.

He put the ball down on the end zone grass. Game over. At last.

Tim got to him first. "You were gonna run it even if we weren't covered, weren't you?"

"Pretty much."

"You're a dog."

Will laughed now.

"Pretty much," he said.

"You need a *real* game, dog," Tim said. "We all do."

Will went back, picked up his ball, staring at it for a second in his hands, like it might have some kind of answer for him.

"Tell me about it," he said.

It was close to six by then and the other guys were rushing home to dinner.

Will was in no rush.

His dinner would be there for him, he knew. His dad always made sure of that. Will didn't know what was on the menu, just that the food would be either in the refrigerator or on the counter, waiting for him to heat it up when he got home.

His dad was already on his way to Newtown by now, where he was taking a class at the community college. Joe Tyler called it a way of getting away from Forbes, even if it was only through books.

So there was no schedule for Will, no set time for him to have his second meal of the day by himself. He walked up Arch Street instead, walked the ten blocks to Forbes High School, wondering if he'd already passed Hannah Grayson's house along the way.

Wishing she had been spying on him today at the end of the game, wishing she'd seen him take it to the house instead of getting brought down by a hole in the ground.

Wondering why he cared what the annoying girl he'd just met thought of him.

He stood on the sidewalk in front of the high school when he got there, looking at the old brick buildings, almost feeling as if he were looking at a picture in some history book. The whole place looked as old and tired to Will as the rest of Forbes did.

Then, ball under his arm, Will walked around back to the football field, the one field in town that was still in decent shape. The wooden scoreboard stared down from one end zone. Wooden bleachers rested empty on both sides of the field. A huge sign stood at the opposite end of the field from the scoreboard. "Home of the Forbes Falcons," the sign read.

Underneath, in fading paint, was a smaller sign, an advertisement that read, "Proudly sponsored by Forbes Flyers, the shoe for fleet feet."

Except that one of the F's was gone, and so it now read "Forbes lyers."

"My dream house," Will said aloud.

No matter how much he fantasized about where his speed, his talent for football, might take him, he knew the path would go through this field.

At this school, in this town, on this side of the river.

He took one last look around, one last good look at his football future, and then began the long walk home.

Cheeseburger tonight.

Cheeseburger and fries and corn on the cob. "A well-balanced meal for a growing boy," his dad said in the note on the fridge. The note also told him there was apple pie for dessert, purchased this afternoon at the Country Cupboard.

Will heated up the food and ate in front of the television set in the living room, watching the end of the six o'clock Sports-Center. He cleaned up when he was done, had two pieces of pie with vanilla ice cream, went upstairs and fired up his laptop so he could check his e-mails again.

There was some junk mail that had gotten through and messages from Tim asking Will to call him later about their upcoming fantasy draft.

That was it.

Not what he was looking for, no miracles tonight.

So he sat there for a while online, checking out some of the NFL stat pages, getting ready for the upcoming fantasy draft. The kids his age in the West River league had decided they might as well have a fantasy league, too, and Will had won it easily the year before. This year he had decided to partner up with Tim, mostly because Tim had begged him.

"You do the work, I'll share the glory," Tim had said.

"But what's in it for *me*?"

"That's a very selfish attitude, if you ask me."

"I didn't," Will had said.

Last year fantasy football had just been pure fun. It seemed more important now, though, if only because this year it might be the only way Will would get to compete with the other kids in the West River league.

Fantasy football was just one more version of a game that had always come naturally to Will. He knew the stats he needed, for selecting a quarterback or running back or wide receiver, were already inside his own head, that he didn't need to look them up online. He knew them by heart.

Like football *was* his heart.

Which was why, for the first time ever, despite how his dad and the rest of Forbes had been struggling for years, Will understood what it was like to be poor. He knew a lot of people were a lot worse off than he was, and Will had never been one to feel sorry for himself. He and his dad had it much better than some people—*most* people—who'd lost their jobs when the sneaker factory closed, people who even now were still looking for steady work. Will had lost his mom, and then a first home, which he barely remembered, but he'd always had football. As though the game was the one constant in his life.

Maybe that was why the idea of losing the upcoming season made *him* feel so lost.

He thought about going back downstairs, seeing if there was anything good on television tonight. He didn't really feel like calling Tim, not wanting to talk to anybody in the mood he was in. So he decided to watch one of his favorite movies, *The Express,* the one about an old Syracuse University football player named Ernie Davis.

As much as Will knew about football history, he didn't know much about Ernie Davis at first, just that he was one of the names on the long list of guys who'd won the Heisman Trophy and that he'd been the first African American to win the award. He came from Elmira, New York, just over the Pennsylvania border, and he'd grown up poor. So when Will watched the movie and learned that Ernie Davis died in the end, died before playing a professional game, it had just about killed *him*. He'd rewatched *The Express* many times since, but he'd always shut it off after Syracuse beat Texas and won the Cotton Bowl and the national championship. Will liked his own ending to the movie better. The happy ending. He wished life could work out that way, too.

He watched the movie tonight and got to the Cotton Bowl part, the part with all the dirty play from the other team, the nasty comments made because Ernie Davis was black, the attempts by the Texas players to hurt him every chance they got. But he kept getting back up until his team won the game and finished off its undefeated season.

The end, Will thought, *the happy end,* as he shut off the movie, hearing his dad's car in the driveway at almost the exact same moment.

He heard the car door slam, went over to the window and looked down and saw his dad limping across their small front lawn to the front door, not looking up, not knowing he was being watched from the upstairs window. Will knew his dad always limped more when he thought nobody was watching.

His dad probably wanted a way different story for his own life. Maybe he wished there was a way to pause his own movie right before those two guys destroyed his knee.

Will stood there wondering if his dad even remembered what it was like to run down the field the way Will had today, as if nothing—and nobody—was ever going to stop him. Wondered if his dad even allowed himself to remember the good parts of his own career or if it hurt too much to remember, the way his knee did.

He went to the top of the stairs now to say hi to Joe Tyler.

"What's good?" his dad said when he looked up and saw Will there, smiling at him, moving to the foot of the stairs with no limp at all, opening his arms for Will to come down and give him a hug.

Will raced down the stairs and did just that.

"*You're* good," Will said, hugging him hard.

07

S ix days later Will's dad delivered the mail, including a letter addressed to Will. Will's breath seemed to get caught in his chest when he saw the return address.

It was from New Balance. Will had written a letter to the CEO of the company after doing some research. It was this, his Hail Mary pass with the clock running out and a whole season *really* on the line, that had kept him secretly hoping for days, the top-secret plan he'd only shared with Tim.

It was a crazy plan, he knew, one that would hopefully end with him and his teammates decked out in New Balance football shoes and jerseys and helmets that they'd provide for the team. A plan that ended with New Balance being their proud sponsor this season the way Forbes Flyers had once been the sponsor of the high school team.

Oh, Will knew it was crazy, all right. But he knew it would

have been crazier *not* to try, to just sit there and feel sorry for himself and do nothing.

He picked New Balance just because he'd always worn their football shoes. He found some e-mail addresses on the Internet, thinking they might be a little sketchy but going with them anyway. Taking no chances, he also got the address of New Balance's corporate offices in Boston and sent an actual letter to Mr. Rob DeMartini, the company's CEO:

> *Dear Mr. DeMartini,*
>
> *My name is Will Tyler and I am twelve years old and live in a place called Forbes, Pennsylvania, near Ohio. I live there with my dad because my mom died when I was two.*
>
> *I am going into the seventh grade and love football more than anything. Except my dad. Last year I scored sixteen rushing touchdowns and my team went to the championship game of our league, the Super Bowl of the West River Football League. We lost to Castle Rock, where they make the bottled water, because I fumbled on our last play of the game.*
>
> *From the time we lost, I have been thinking about getting a rematch with Castle Rock. That brings me to the purpose of my letter, which is that we're probably not going to get a chance at a rematch or a chance to even compete for one because there's not enough money in our town's budget. Our season is ending before it even starts.*

Since you make New Balance shoes, you might know that we used to make Forbes Flyers here (not "we" like in my family, even though my grandfather and father worked there) before the company went out of business and the factory closed. Little by little, all of Forbes seems to be closing, too. Now it looks as if my teammates and I might be out of business because Forbes can't afford football anymore for guys our age.

So I was wondering:

Do you think you might possibly sponsor my team this season?

I don't know how we could repay the money it would cost—ten thousand dollars—except by trying to do New Balance proud in the way we would play.

Nobody knows I am writing this letter to you, not even my dad. He's a proud man and doesn't like taking charity. He works hard every day. But I don't think of this as asking for charity. I think of it as asking for a chance. A chance to work hard at the game I love.

Mr. DeMartini, my teammates and I feel like we got hit from the blind side. But my dad once told me it takes no talent to get knocked down, especially in a game like football. He said that it's how you get back up that counts. I am asking for your help, to give me and my teammates a chance to get back up. If you do, I will make you a promise in return:

We will be a team that will make you stand up and cheer.

Maybe we can even get our town to do the same thing.

They could use it here.

Thank you very much for taking the time to read this letter. My dad has always told me to speak from the heart and that is what I tried to do.

Very respectfully yours,

Will Tyler

Now he was staring at the return address on the letter he held now in hands that didn't shake this way when a game was on the line:

> New Balance Headquarters
> 20 Guest Street
> Brighton, Mass. 02135-2088

Will was careful opening the envelope, even though his first impulse was to rip it open like it was a Christmas present. He knew that if somehow there was good news inside, he was going to want to keep everything intact.

The letter was typed, with Mr. DeMartini's signature at the bottom:

Dear Will,

As you can probably guess, we get a lot of letters at New Balance asking us for money, from people all over the world. But I'm not sure I've ever received one that touched me quite like yours did, like it came straight from your heart to mine.

And like me, you've probably seen the credit card commercials on TV where they give the dollar value on a few items and then have something at the end that they call "priceless."

Well, I'm pretty sure that when I was your age, I would have considered my own football season priceless.

That's why I consider having to pay only ten thousand dollars for yours a bargain.

Jim Davis, our chairman, is an old Middlebury College football player, and we've both always shared a dream of owning a National Football League team. That may be a little out of our reach. But when I showed him your letter, he said maybe it was about time New Balance owned a football team, even if it was one in Forbes, Pa.

Somebody from my office will contact your dad in the next few days and he can give us the proper contacts to start working out all the details of sponsoring a team in your league.

For now?

Go tell your friends and your coach and the whole town if you want to that there's going to be a season after all.

I can't tell you how much I look forward to meeting you
one of these days. Maybe at the championship game.
I look forward to watching you carry the ball.

                                    Your new friend in football,
                                        Rob DeMartini

Will was by himself. When his dad had delivered the mail, he had just rung the doorbell like he always did, turned and waved when he saw Will waving at him from his bedroom window. Then he took a right at the end of the walk and headed up Valley to continue his route.

No limping today, not with Will watching him.

Will had raced downstairs—having a feeling and not knowing why—saw the letter, saw who it was from, took it into the kitchen and sat down at the table to read it.

He read every word and then when he finished, he went back and read the whole thing again, just to make sure that he hadn't dreamed up the whole thing.

His heart was pounding as if he'd just gone the whole length of the field on a kickoff return, had just crossed the goal line.

He took a deep breath, trying to calm himself, trying to be cool.

Then he raised his right arm nearly to the ceiling, fist closed, pulled his arm down hard, the way Hannah Grayson had done after she made that insane kick in front of him.

"*Yes!*" he shouted at the top of his voice, not caring whether the neighbors could hear him or not.

Then: *"Yesyesyes!"*

And this time he did the kind of crazy touchdown dance he never did on the field, dancing around the small kitchen like a complete lunatic, banging his hip on the corner of the table and not caring.

Not sure in the moment whether to laugh or cry.

There was going to be a team.

There was going to be a season.

He thought: *Sometimes a running back can complete a Hail Mary pass after all.*

He tried to call Tim, got his machine. Same with Chris Aiello. *Forget it,* he thought, *I'll get on my bike and go tell them to their faces.* He would tell it to all his teammates even if it took all day.

A team and a season and new uniforms and cleats and real games after all.

Yesyesyes!

Will left the letter and the envelope on the table, ran out the front door, took the same right up Valley that his dad had taken, knowing the route by heart from all the days when he'd walked it with Joe Tyler.

He was glad that Tim and Chris weren't home, now that he thought about it, running at full speed to catch up with his dad.

His dad should be the first one to know that it was still all right to believe in miracles.

Even in Forbes, Pennsylvania.

08

W ill didn't expect his dad to jump for joy when he caught up with him at the corner of Cherry and Elm, not on that knee, but he thought he'd be more excited.

But when Will gave him the news, the first thing he said was, "Ironic, isn't it? One of the companies that put this town out of business is now saving a town football team."

At first Will thought he might just be trying to be funny, but he wasn't. Will could tell by his eyes.

"But, Dad," Will said, "the important thing is that Mr. De-Martini stepped up to the plate for us. You can read his letter when you get home. He sounds like a great guy."

His dad leaned against a tree. "Bud, don't get me wrong, I'm happy for you. I am. It was killing me, too, thinking of you losing a season from your life. Because you're never sure how many of those you're going to get." He turned his head and looked down Elm, like he was trying to see all the way to the end of it, all the way to the river. "Trust me, I found that out the hard way."

"It's all right if I go tell some of the guys, right?" Will said. "He's not gonna change his mind? Or do you think I should make some kind of announcement at school tomorrow?"

"That's a lot of questions."

Will grinned. "Answer them in any order."

"Go tell your guys," Joe Tyler said. "Some sneaker companies you can probably trust not to bail out on you. Trust them to do what they say they're going to do."

Will put out his fist and his dad pounded it with his own.

"Dad," he said, smiling, "I did it."

"You did."

"You always tell me it's not about getting knocked down, it's how you get back up, right?"

"Right as rain."

"Well, I wouldn't let the town council take me down and keep me down."

Joe Tyler messed up Will's hair and said, "That's your mom in you coming out. She was the toughest person I ever knew." Then he said to his son, "Listen, the mail in this bag isn't going to deliver itself today. So you go do what the big sneaker man told you to do, and tell your good news to anybody you want to."

Will did his best to hug his dad around the large mailbag on his shoulder, and then ran back home to get his bike. As he came through the front door, he heard the phone.

He ran to the kitchen and checked the caller ID and saw that it was Ben Clark calling from Castle Rock.

The two of them hadn't talked all summer and for a second, Will wondered how he could possibly know about New Balance.

"Hey, man," Ben said, "I heard the news."

Will said, "What news would that be?"

"About your team. Bummer."

Will smiled, thinking: *The* old *news. The old bad news.*

"Listen," Ben said, "lemme talk for a second before you say anything." He was a quarterback and quarterbacks always thought everybody else should shut up and listen. "I was talking to our coach and we agree you should come play for us. He said he'd even drive you over sometimes if your dad was working or whatever. You know I've been telling you since the championship game that you should be playing for us. Dude, imagine what it would be like if you got to play half your games on that field turf of ours. It would be, like, *epic.*"

"Listen," Will said. "You're nice to offer."

Ready to tell him no, but not about Mr. DeMartini's letter. He wasn't about to tell the Castle Rock quarterback that news before he told any of his teammates.

But then Ben was talking again.

"It not just a nice offer," he said. "We're treating you like a free agent that just fell into our laps. My coach was saying how they're always talking about contracting the poor teams in the NBA. He goes, 'Will's team just got contracted.'"

And for that one moment, Will *did* picture himself on that field turf they'd put in new last season. In that moment, Will wasn't trying to imagine what he'd look like in whatever uniforms New Balance was going to buy but in the cool Castle Rock uniforms that they'd worn last season, the bottled-water company having not spared any expense in styling them up.

Mostly Will imagined himself running behind that huge offensive line of theirs, not having to do it all himself, the defense not able to stack up against him because they had to worry about Ben Clark's golden arm.

Yeah, he thought, phone in his hand, neither he nor Ben saying anything.

It would be epic.

Then he looked over at the kitchen table where he'd left Rob DeMartini's letter.

"I have a team," he said finally.

"But I thought—"

Now Will was the one doing the interrupting.

"You're a couple of days behind the news," Will said. "We came up with the money."

Nearly saying, *I* came up with the money.

"In *Forbes*?" Ben said.

He couldn't have sounded more surprised if Will had told him he'd found ten thousand dollars under his bed.

"How?" Ben asked.

"Long story," Will said. "But as stories go, pretty stellar. Tell you about it the next time I see you."

"You're really gonna have a team?" Ben Clark said. "Because

my dad went to the coaches' meeting with Coach Tate last night, and he said the league's pretty much resigned to going with seven teams this season instead of eight."

"It'll be eight," Will said. "We're in."

"Well, congrats," Ben said. "I guess."

"You guess?"

"Dude," Ben said, "you guys barely had eleven to suit up last season. You bringing in some kind of big recruiting class now?"

Will knew what a good guy Ben Clark was. What Tim called a bro. Not spoiled or stuck up like he could have been. Will knew Ben was just playing. But he knew something else: it had only taken a few seconds for him to go from a friend back to being an opponent.

"We'll be all right," Will said.

He thought of saying it as *aiight*, but every time he tried that, he just sounded—and felt—like a tool.

"Well, we'll see how all right you're gonna be when they make the schedule," Ben said. "Game'll be at your place in the regular season this year."

"Who knows," Will said, "maybe the championship game will be here, too."

"Oh, so you're going from having no team to getting home field in the playoffs? If you count that junkyard as a field."

"You never know."

"In your dreams, Tyler."

Then they were both laughing, chirping back and forth a little

more, before Will said he had to be someplace. But before he
hung up, he said, "Ben? Thanks for calling and asking. No lie."

"You still belong with us, whether you've got a team over
there or not."

"Nah," Will said. "I'm right where I belong."

Something he never would have said before he picked up the
mail today.

Then he hung up and got on his bike.

Ben Clark had to be kidding, worrying that they weren't going
to have enough guys who wanted to play over on this side of the
river. In their own cool uniforms? With their cool New Balance
football shoes?

Every kid in school would want in.

Or so he thought.

09

By the end of the first week of school Will had only found ten guys his age who wanted to play football in Forbes this season.

On a scale of ten?

He felt like a zero, felt almost as bad as he did when he thought there was going to be no season.

The worst part?

The team had no coach.

Mr. Carrington, who worked at the Bank of Forbes, had coached the twelve-year-old team in town for as long as Will could remember. And Mr. Carrington had agreed to do it again this season, at least before the town council had spread the news about not having enough money. But when Will and Tim stopped by the bank on Monday to tell him about New Balance, tell him they were going to have a season after all, he heard a different kind of bad news.

Mr. Carrington had gotten a better job at a bank called Fifth Third, in Toledo, Ohio. It had all happened so quickly, but it was too good of an opportunity to pass up. He said that his wife and kids had already moved so that they could start school on time.

Mr. Carrington said he felt terrible telling them like this, that he hadn't bothered to tell the kids on the team or even the town council, because he didn't think there was going to *be* a team. Said he'd been away for most of the last couple of weeks looking for a house to buy in Toledo.

"As great an opportunity as this is, I honestly feel terrible about leaving you guys," Mr. Carrington said. "And once Bobby hears the news, he's going to feel worse than I do. This has been hard enough on him already."

So that's why none of the guys had seen Bobby lately. Their quarterback had moved to Toledo.

No coach, no quarterback. Just like that. Not even Troy Palomalu could sack that many people with one hit. Now the week had come to an end—amazingly, at least to Will's way of thinking—with them being one player short of being able to call themselves a real team. Will had thrown up his prayer and New Balance had answered it . . . except it turned out they only had ten live bodies in a sport where you needed eleven.

So now Will and Tim and Chris and Jeremiah were sitting on the floor of Will's bedroom, an emergency summit of the core players on the team. They had all chipped in to order pizza.

"It's a good thing we have food," Tim said. "I don't think nearly as well when I'm hungry."

"Then how do we explain the way you think the rest of the time?" Will asked.

Tim neatly folded the slice of pepperoni in his hand and said, "Why do you have to be such a hater?"

There hadn't been much talking while they waited for the pizza to be delivered. Their initial enthusiasm over the letter, the excitement of spreading the news that Mr. DeMartini and New Balance were willing to finance their team and their season had been replaced now by the very bad vibe they all had now because of the *lack* of enthusiasm shown by the rest of the seventh grade when it came to football.

Before the letter came, Will had thought the only number he had to worry about was ten thousand dollars.

Not ten players.

They had all talked up the team to their classmates. They had posted a sign-up sheet and had everyone on the team add their name to get the ball rolling. Ten names on Tuesday.

By Friday?

The same ten names.

One kid from last year's team, Carlos Estrada, had decided he wanted to play soccer this year, not football. "Where?" Will asked him. "On what team?"

"Castle Rock."

"Dude, you're killing me," Will said.

But there was no talking him out of it. Carlos had been a soccer player growing up in the Dominican Republic and he was happy to be playing again.

So he was gone and Bobby Carrington was gone, and thirteen had become eleven. Brendon Donelson, their center from last season, was the next to go. He had broken his arm at the skateboard park over in Castle Rock at the beginning of August and was still in a cast. He was just hoping he'd be ready for basketball season.

Ten guys. Nobody new wanted to play.

It was beyond amazing to Will.

"You sure you talked to everybody?" Chris Aiello said.

"I talked to every jock in the middle school," Will said. "I talked to baseball players, basketball players, I even tried to hijack some of Carlos's new friends on the soccer team. Nothing."

"We just have to find one more guy," Tim said. "How hard can that be?"

Will said, "How hard can it be? Let me ask you something: how we lookin' so far, big boy?"

There was another long silence while they ate. Every so often you would hear the sound of Tim's cell phone buzzing. He was the only one of them who had one. Will wondered who could be calling him when his best buds were right here in this room.

"And think about it," Will said. "Say we do find another guy. We're gonna try to play the whole season with eleven? Really? What if somebody gets hurt? We're right back to where we are right now. I can see it now: Mr. DeMartini shows up to see us play only we don't that day, because it turns out to be a stinking forfeit."

"They wouldn't have this problem in Castle Rock," Tim said. "They have to *cut* kids over there."

"Not just football country over there," Will said. "A whole different football planet."

He could hear Ben Clark's voice inside his head again, clear as a bell, right after Will told him they had the money for the team and Ben had said, "In *Forbes*?"

Will started to take a bite of pizza, then tossed his slice into the box, no longer hungry. The week he'd just had felt like a whole game of hard hits. And he still couldn't believe they were in this kind of fix. It had been a perfect plan. As Tim loved to say, Will felt as if he'd absolutely crushed the whole idea of getting their team back together.

Now this.

"We gotta figure something out," he said.

"You know what this all means? That we drove the ball down the field and couldn't push it across."

Will turned and glared at him, but Tim gave him a wave-off, standing up now, not just addressing Will, addressing the whole group.

"Let me finish," he said. "And by the way? That glare of death from you doesn't scare me nearly as much as it used to." He took a deep breath. "Okay, we've been all over the place tonight. I think what we need to do right now is prioritize."

Will couldn't help it; as frustrated and angry as he was feeling, he barked out a laugh.

"You don't even know what that means," he said.

"Do too," Tim said. "I made my mother use it in a sentence at breakfast." He said to Will, "Do I have your permission to continue?"

Will nodded.

"This is only my opinion, but before we think about finding another player, I think we have to make sure we've got somebody to coach us. Because they won't let us play in the league without a coach, even if we get to eleven."

He sat back down then, picked up the slice that Will had just dropped into the box and said, "You gonna finish this?"

"Okay, so let's talk about coaches," Will said.

They sat there and began to go through the list of possibilities. "What about Mr. York?" Chris said. Mr. York had coached them last year. Maybe they could talk him into moving up and coaching them, if somebody else could coach the elevens.

Will said, "You didn't hear? He moved to Castle Rock and took a job in the bottle factory, some kind of night manager."

"Never mind," Chris said.

Jeremiah said, "What about Mr. Pags? He played in college, right?"

Mr. Pagliarulo was their phys ed teacher at Forbes Middle. But he was also their math teacher and everyone knew his idea of teaching phys ed was handing his kids a few basket- or soccer balls, taking his whistle and sitting on the bleachers grading homework.

Then they talked about their dads.

Will said his couldn't do it, no way, not holding down his post office job and going to night school. Will had always thought his dad would make a great coach but knew he wouldn't want to do it, would rather do just about anything than get back on a football field. That's why Will wasn't even going to ask, knowing how bad his dad would feel when he said no.

Tim's dad was also ruled out instantly. The guys knew he was constantly traveling back and forth between Forbes and Pittsburgh, where he'd landed temp work as a computer technician, hoping it would eventually lead to a full-time job. Will didn't even want to think about what would happen if Mr. LeBlanc got his wish and had to move.

Chris's dad was an interstate truck driver and was usually gone for half the week and sometimes more. Jeremiah's parents had divorced after the sneaker factory closed and his dad had left town not long after that, taking an assembly-line job in Detroit for one of the car companies.

"Maybe if some of the dads took *turns* coaching," Chris said.

In that moment Will felt like he was a D lineman with a big hand up, swatting a pass out of the air.

"We're desperate," he said to Chris. "But not that desperate. At least not yet. Coaching by committee? It would feel like they were babysitting us."

"Why don't you coach?" Tim said to Will. "Seriously, dude. You know more about football than any five kids I know. Or any of us know. And more than most adults."

"This isn't a book," Will said.

Wishing it were.

Thinking about the happy endings you got in the sports books he loved. Sitting there in his bedroom and thinking about the happy ending he thought he had—or at least the beginning of one—when he'd opened Mr. DeMartini's letter.

They heard the front door close, Will's dad giving them a shout-out from the bottom of the stairs. Then Will could hear the slow walk up the stairs he had heard so many times before, almost being able to time when his dad would finally get to the top.

Joe Tyler poked his head in, saw the scatter of pizza boxes and empty Gatorade bottles. "I assume," he said, surveying the mess with one raised eyebrow, "that you gentlemen are going to clean up when you're done."

"On it, Mr. T.," Tim said.

"I actually meant the other guys, Timmy. Tragically I gave up on your cleanup abilities long ago."

Tim put his head down, trying to look sad. "A family of haters," he said.

Will's dad said, "Any progress?"

He knew what the summit was about, knew the spot they were all in; Will had been giving his dad the play-by-play all week long.

"Nope," Will said. "Not unless you count knocking off two large pies and still not coming up with one more player, or one coach."

"You'll think of something, you always do," Joe Tyler said.

Will said, "You sound like him." Nodding at Tim.

Joe Tyler grinned and said, "Watch your mouth." Paused and said, "Seriously? Look on the bright side. You wouldn't even be here tonight if you hadn't come up with the brilliant idea of sending the letter to the sneaker guy."

"I know, Dad. Believe me, I *know.* But I was sure that when guys found out that not only were we gonna have a team, that we had a sponsor—"

"A *proud* sponsor," Tim added.

"—like New Balance, guys would be willing to run through a wall to play with us."

His dad said, "You've never had to run through walls because you always found a way to make a hole for yourself, even when the blocking broke down. Or found a hole. So find one now."

His dad made it sound so easy. Will wished. The guys helped him clean up. Then they left, too. It was still way earlier than when Will went to bed, especially on a weekend night. But sometimes thinking this hard, on anything, thinking this hard and wanting something this badly, exhausted him in a way that sports never did.

He washed up, got ready for bed, shut off the lights, found the Pirates station on his small radio, knowing they were getting ready to play the Padres in San Diego. Will liked baseball well enough. But he *loved* games from the West Coast in the night.

So now that was his background music, the voices of the Pirates announcers, the sounds of the game coming into his bedroom from all the way across the country.

But he was still thinking football thoughts, back of his head on the pillow, fingers laced behind it, staring at the ceiling.

Waiting for another brilliant idea.

Trying to find his hole.

T his time he wasn't going to tell anybody what he planned to do, not even Tim. He was just going to improvise, the way you did with a broken play.

He had decided in the night that Tim was wrong, that his first priority was to find more bodies, not a coach, even though he was pretty much set on who he thought the coach ought to be. It was actually pretty funny, Will thought. Not *Simpsons* funny. Just odd. Just by writing a letter and getting a response he never expected, it was like he was now running football for twelve-year-olds in Forbes. Like he was the town council guy for the West River league.

And all he really wanted to do was have somebody hand him the ball.

For now, he was keeping his eye on the ball.

Somehow—whatever it took—he kept repeating that one line to himself, over and over—they were going to have a season.

Somehow, he had been telling himself all night and all morning and would keep telling himself, he was going to find at least
one more guy. Had decided that was job one, as his dad liked to
say. If they had to start the season with eleven, so be it, they'd
just line up and pray that nobody got hurt. Or quit. Will had
come too far to back up or back off now.

Whatever it took.

Of course he'd never heard of a team going into a season with
just eleven players. Of course he knew enough about football to
know how they'd be living on the edge every time the ball was
snapped. Oh, sure, he could see it now, some close game where
their best guys would never get to come off the field. That part
was fine for Will, of course, he never wanted to be off the field
for a single play. He even loved playing on the kickoff team and
flying downfield as a gunner covering punt returns. But not
everybody was like him. They just weren't. He knew his friends
loved football, just not the way he did.

So it wasn't too hard to see Tim or Chris or Jeremiah being
totally gassed by the end of some games, especially when the
weather was still warm in September, hands on knees, too tired
to make the tackle or the block or the play that might make the
difference between winning and losing.

Because that was Will Tyler's big thing, even though he hadn't
been talking about it with his buds; they had other things to
worry about these days. But he didn't just want to have a season. He wanted to *win* the season. For him, the object of the

game hadn't changed since last year's championship game against Castle Rock:

.To beat them in the big game.

To do that, he knew he needed more bodies.

Starting with one more, just because you had to start somewhere.

It was why he got on his bike on Saturday morning and went looking for the biggest body in the seventh grade at Forbes Middle School.

Toby Keenan, who looked like he was two or three years older than he was—or more—lived in a small one-story house on the far side of town away from the river, his street becoming a dirt road at the end where the house was.

Toby lived there with his dad, who'd been a teammate of Will's dad at Forbes High School, a middle linebacker on defense and a guard on offense.

"But his real positions were mean and scary," Joe Tyler said.

Now Dick Keenan worked for the town of Forbes, not for the town council, the way Tim's dad did, but a guy who did road work and tree work in the summer and drove a snowplow in the winter, clearing roads for the town and driveways on his own time. Dick Keenan was big himself, with a huge belly and a look on his face, every time Will saw him behind the wheel of one of his trucks, that made you think that in the very next moment he was going to pick a fight with the whole world.

Will didn't know a whole lot about Mr. Keenan's wife, even had trouble remembering what she looked like when she was still living with them. Basically he just knew that she wasn't living with them now, that she was another person who had left Forbes and never come back.

Will had asked his dad one time why Mrs. Keenan had left her husband and son behind and all his dad said was, "The reason was Mr. Keenan."

When Forbes was still playing in Pop Warner, the last year they played in Pop Warner, Toby had played in fifth grade, as a middle linebacker, just like his dad. He and Tim were about the same size then; it was before Toby just shot up past everybody in their grade. One time Mr. Pags had looked out at the gym floor during phys ed and said, "Sometimes I think I can *hear* Toby growing."

But Toby could play. They put him at middle linebacker and had him play some tight end, didn't even look at him anywhere else, just because of his size. And he wasn't just a load, he could run, even if he seemed reluctant—at least in Will's view—to really lay people out on defense; sometimes the coaches had to remind him that it was a contact sport and hard tackling was allowed.

But when he did put a hard tackle on you in practice, as Will found out more than once, it was about the same as running into a tree.

Everybody could see he had a talent for football and two

things going for him that Will's dad always said you couldn't teach:

Big and scary fast.

Toby Keenan just seemed almost too gentle a kid for football. Maybe that's why, Will's view again, he never loved playing. And that would have been enough right there to hold him back, but there was something much bigger going on for the big kid:

His dad.

Forget about loving the game; in the end Dick Keenan made his son hate it.

Mr. Keenan came to most games, home and away, a permanent game face on him, one that reminded Will of a balled fist. That wasn't the worst of it, either, the worst of it was that he yelled almost the whole time. Yelled out more than even the coaches did. More than the other parents combined.

At home games, Will would look up into the stands sometimes and it would be the same scene, over and over again:

Mr. Keenan at the top of the bleachers, by himself, yelling away. By the time they had played just a couple of games, most of the other parents wouldn't go near him. And any adult showing up for the first time wouldn't stay near him for long.

He never swore, not that Will heard. He didn't make negative comments about the other players, on either team. Never complained about the officiating.

It was all directed at Toby.

Telling him to pay attention. To know where the ball was. To be aware of whatever formation the other team was running. Telling all this to a fifth-grade middle linebacker.

"Don't be a bonehead and go for that fake, you jack wagon. How about hitting somebody, or do you still think you're playing *flag* football?"

Every so often, maybe once or twice a game, he would offer his son what passed for a compliment with him:

"That's better."

About halfway through the season their coach that year, Mr. Mallozzi, asked Toby's dad if he could possibly dial it down a little. This was after a game, in the parking lot, and the whole team heard and saw what happened next, Mr. Keenan almost challenging Mr. Mallozzi to a fight.

It ended with Mr. Keenan saying, "I don't tell you how to coach, don't tell me how to father."

So nothing changed until the last game, what was called their Super Bowl. Late in the game, a game Forbes was winning by twenty points, Toby missed a tackle on the other team's tight end and the kid went sixty-five yards for a touchdown that only made the final score a little closer than it should have been.

For some reason, it made Mr. Keenan's head explode one more time that afternoon.

As soon as the tight end was across the goal line, this is what everybody at Shea Field heard:

"Toby Keenan, if you're not gonna play to the end of the game, why are you still out there?"

There was a pause and then:

"Why don't you just quit playing now?"

That's exactly what Toby Keenan did.

He walked off the field before the kickoff. Took off his helmet when he got to the sideline, took off his jersey, put both at the end of the Forbes bench. Then he walked past the bleachers, his dad at his usual spot near the top, kept walking toward the parking lot.

And as far as Will knew, Toby walked all the way home, to the house on the dirt road that was the end of Spencer Street. He had never come out for football or played football, not even flag football, since.

Now Will was about to knock on his front door and ask him to come back.

The orange Department of Public Works truck was in the yard. Next to it was an old maroon Camry. It had to mean that Mr. Keenan was home. Will didn't see as how that was going to help him out very much. He'd made the bike ride over here thinking he had a better chance of pulling this off—how many Hail Mary passes could you throw?—if it was just him and Toby alone.

Toby answered the door, and as soon as Will saw him, he was thinking that the only thing this boy had in common with Dick Keenan was size, because he had a much nicer face, with much darker hair, worn long.

Will had always thought there was a niceness about Toby

at school, as shy and quiet as he was, as much as he kept to himself.

He must have gotten that from his mom. Briefly Will thought of all the things his own dad said Will had in common with *his* mom, the one who'd left him a lot differently than Toby's had.

"Hey," Toby said.

"Hey," Will said.

Keeping his voice as low as possible, Toby said, "Listen, I know why you're here."

Will smiled. "He reads minds, too."

Still standing there on the porch, Toby having made no move to invite him in.

It was then that Will heard the booming, familiar voice from somewhere behind Toby, like the voice was trying to rattle the walls of the tiny house, like the voice was still coming from the top of the bleachers.

"Who's here?" Mr. Keenan yelled. "Is it that idiot cable guy finally showing up three hours after he was supposed to be here?"

Then Mr. Keenan was standing behind his son, in his white undershirt and baggy jeans, looking disappointed when he saw that their visitor was Will.

Nobody was very happy to see Will at 127 Spencer.

"I know you," he said. "Joe Tyler's kid. The halfback. You're fast."

"Nice to see you, Mr. Keenan."

"Check him out, Tobes," the dad said. "A pip-squeak half your size and still twice the player you are. Or *were.*"

"Dad," Toby said.

A look on his face that Will remembered from when they still played together.

The big man put his small eyes on Will and said, "What do you want?"

To get as far away from here as possible, Will thought, *as soon as I say to Toby what I came here to say.*

"Just came to see Toby."

"Never saw you here before."

In the same soft voice he'd used when he greeted Will, eyes down like he was studying his sneakers, or Will's, Toby said, "He's my friend, Dad. He doesn't need a reason to be here."

They all just stood there until Mr. Keenan said to Toby, "Well, anyway, when the cable guy shows up, come get me even if I'm taking my nap, so I can give him a piece of my mind."

Will found himself wondering how big a piece Toby's dad could spare as the man grumped off toward the back of the house.

When he was gone, Toby said, "I'd ask you to come in. But you don't want to."

Will said, "Yeah."

"It's cool," Toby said. "I'm used to it."

They both knew what he was talking about.

"Yeah," Will said again.

Toby said, "You should probably go, though. If he figures out why you came—at least why I'm pretty sure you came—it won't be good."

"I'm not here about him," Will said. "I'm here about you."

Now Toby's voice was barely more than a whisper, the sound coming out of him more scared than anything else. "Will," he said. "I wish I could. But I can't."

Will tried to look past him, saying, "Maybe you can't." *It's like we're talking in code,* he thought. "But what you *can* do is hear me out. Out here or inside, your call, but I gotta say what I came to say."

Toby pointed and the two of them walked to the end of the driveway where the truck was parked and sat next to each other on the rear fender, almost like they were using the orange truck for cover.

"Listen, I'll try to keep this short," Will said. "I'm not here to blow smoke at you, but I'm not gonna lie, either. We need more players, like right now; practice is starting in a week. So I need you to play. But on top of that, I *want* you to play, too."

"But I told you. I can't."

"Can't or won't?"

"Does it make a difference?"

Then he took a casual look over his shoulder, at the front door, the door still closed, Dick Keenan at a safe distance, at least for now.

"Dude," Will said. "This season is going to be *awesome*. With you back in uniform, we can kick some serious butt. Shock the world!" He grinned. "Well, maybe not the world, just the West River league. But we can *do* this. Turn ourselves into one of those underdog teams. Heck, not just one of them. Make ourselves *the* underdogs. Do something that will make this town remember what it's like to cheer."

"You don't need me to do that."

"See, that's just one more thing you're wrong about. We do need you. Need your size, your speed. The way you play, adding you to the guys we already have, we *can* crush this, I totally mean it."

Trying to talk himself into that, he knew, as much as Toby Keenan.

"You mean the way I played. Like, past tense."

"I don't know everything at our age, but I know this: you don't lose it between ten and twelve, dude. So you missed last season. Big deal. You're a great player. Maybe the other guys didn't see it. Maybe even the coaches didn't. But I did. You'd barely figured out how to put on your own shoulder pads, and you were still one of the best guys we had."

"It doesn't matter."

Will said, "Are you serious? It's *all* that matters."

Toby gave another quick look over his shoulder. "Will," he said. "You love to play. I didn't. I *don't*. And probably never will."

"Because you haven't given yourself a chance." Will nodded at the house. "Because *he* never gave you a chance."

"It wasn't all him. It was me, too. And I was never as good as you say I was."

Will made a buzzer noise.

"Wrong again."

Now Will checked the front door, lowered his own voice. "You're listening to me, but you're not *hearing* me. I saw what you were like in practice when he wasn't around. I saw what it was like for you when he didn't show up at an away game. You were one player when he was around and a totally different one when he wasn't."

Toby said, "You don't understand." Like his own words were hurting him. "If I come back, he comes back. Are you gonna tell me you want that?"

Will gave him a long look. "I would make that deal in a heartbeat," he said. "Then come back an hour later and make it again."

Then the words were just spilling out of him, Will telling Toby they would have beaten Castle Rock last season if he'd still been playing, still in the middle of the D. Telling him how much they needed him, not just because he would make a total of eleven players, because they needed his talent.

Needed somebody his size, because even though Will could imagine a team that was good and fast, they were going to get pushed around without at least one big guy the other team had to worry about.

"And not just big in size," Will said. "But with a big heart. Like yours. Like the one I know you have to have just to . . . just to *be.*"

"It's not what *he* says," Toby said. "He talks about me like I'm the opposite, because I quit and wouldn't go back. Said I wasn't just heartless, that I was gutless."

For the first time, Toby smiled. "Maybe my dad thinks he's the only one with guts, because *his* gut is so gigantic."

Toby Keenan looked down again, the smile off his face, out of him, that fast. "But why are we even talking about this?" he said. "It would just start up all over again."

"Only if you let it. Only if you let *him*."

"It's like they say on TV. You can't stop him, you can only hope to contain him."

Then: "You don't know what it's like."

Will said, "You're right, I don't. But I will make you a promise: you won't just be getting a bunch of teammates who will have your back, you will be getting a bunch of friends. Starting with me." Will kept going, feeling like he had his attention, like he might be getting through. Might be on a roll all of a sudden. "Get it through your head: you wouldn't be doing this to prove anything to your dad. But maybe it would be about proving something to yourself. There's a big player inside you, no matter what you're telling yourself. Let him out."

Will told Toby he didn't need an answer today. And if he wanted, Will told him, he could come and watch the first couple of practices, no pressure, no worries, just to check it all out, just see what it felt like to be around the game again.

Toby said he'd think about it, that was the best he could do.

Before adding this: "But it's still not gonna happen."

"Give the idea a chance," Will said. "All I'm asking."

"Thanks," Toby said.

"For what?"

Toby said, "Just thanks."

They pounded each other some fist. Will walked down the driveway to where he'd left his bike. Before he got on, he turned and saw Toby Keenan walking slowly toward the house, as if it was the last place on earth he wanted to be.

Like he was walking off the field that day, walking away from football the way he did two years ago.

Will watched until he was through the front door, closing it behind him, Will feeling bad for him, for the life he had on the other side of that door.

He was still glad he'd come.

The big kid hadn't said yes.

But he sure hadn't said no.

11

He briefly thought about going straight home then, calling it a day, calling Tim when he got there, maybe some of the other guys, trying to get up a game at Shea later. Then maybe go into town and get some ice cream at Scoop, a place Will knew had been in Forbes even before the sneaker factory.

"Homemade ice cream at Scoop when I was a boy, homemade now," his dad often said. "At least Ben and Jerry and Baskin and Robbins didn't wipe them out the way the big sneaker companies wiped out the Flyers."

But Will convinced himself he might be on a little bit of a roll here. He'd left Toby's house believing that the guy still wanted to play. That he *did* want to come back, whether his dad came along with him—at the top of his voice—or not.

So he decided he wasn't going to wait for the perfect moment or wait until tomorrow, he was going to recruit himself a coach right now; it couldn't be any harder than trying to get Toby turned around.

Getting Toby to listen when Will started talking to *him* from the heart.

On his way through town, Will did stop at Scoop after all, ordered himself a black-and-white shake because he'd brought just enough money for one with him.

He sat and drank it at the end of the counter, trying to rehearse his speech a little more, knowing he was probably only going to get one shot at this.

That meant, one shot to get it right. And maybe *Tim* was right, maybe he did think better if he wasn't trying to do it on an empty stomach.

When he finished the shake, he got back on his bike, ready to roll in all ways. If Will Tyler knew one thing, it was this: he was pretty honest with himself. So maybe he was just being a dreamer all over again, about all of it, maybe Toby was only being polite, he had no intention of playing, he just wanted Will to leave. And leave him alone.

A definite possibility.

But Will always chose to believe in the best possibilities, even when he was down. There'd never been a time in football when he thought a play wasn't going to work before the ball was snapped. Even last season, the championship game against Castle Rock, Will knowing that there really wasn't enough time to come all the way back, he kept telling himself and his teammates that there was.

He'd waited behind Bobby Carrington and seen himself taking the handoff from him and breaking into the clear, going all the way, recovering the onside kick that would come next. Coming all the way back the way the Eagles did later in the same season against the Giants, that game right before Christmas when they were behind 31–10 with seven-and-a-half minutes left and then scored the last twenty-eight points, the last touchdown coming when DeSean Jackson—who had the kind of speed even Will only had in his *dreams*—took a punt return all the way to the house as time expired.

"As long as there's still time," DeSean Jackson said that day, "you can't give up."

So Will wasn't even close to giving up yet, on the season or on Toby or getting the coach he wanted, the coach he knew would be perfect for his underdog team. What did his dad always say?

If you don't think you can, you can't.

Will rode his bike to the house and waited.

He was sitting there on his windowsill when he saw the guy he wanted to be his coach finally show up.

Saw Joe Tyler move slowly and painfully up the walk, limping more than usual today, worse than ever, limping so badly that he didn't even try to fake it when he looked up and saw Will waving at him.

His dad had been at the gym.

Even after a week when he'd mostly delivered the mail on foot, he still dragged himself to the gym on the weekends, sometimes both days, trying to gut his way through the exercises the physical therapist had given him. Somehow trying to make the knee stronger, build up the muscles around it, doing everything he could to stay away from something his doctor and the therapist had told him was probably inevitable:

Knee replacement surgery.

Joe Tyler fought that idea even harder than going back to a factory job.

"There are two words that would never go together with me," he told Will. "*Elective* and *surgery*."

"But I was with you when Dr. Friedman said that the operation would improve the quality of your life," Will had said.

Even now he could remember the look his dad shot him when he said that, smiling, but his eyes sad. Will knew those sad eyes; he'd see them on his dad sometimes when he'd look at pictures of Will's mom.

"Quality of life?" he'd said. "It would take more than a knee operation."

Now he was stretched out on the couch, ice pack on the knee, Will having brought him a tall glass of lemonade, his dad doing what he always did when he got back from the gym, asking out loud, not really even talking to Will, why he bothered, he always felt worse when he got home, would probably feel even worse when he had to get up and do it again tomorrow.

And worse than that on Monday when it was time to get back to work.

"I wouldn't even know what good felt like," he said, "if good ever did come along.

"Maybe, in my next life," he said to Will, "I'll get to sit down once in a while during my workweek."

He looked up at Will, standing over the couch, and said, "And what's on your mind?"

"Nothing."

"Sure there is. It's written all over your face." He winced when he shifted his position and moved the ice pack a little. "You're a great son. Great ballplayer. Truly terrible liar."

"Gee," Will said, "I never heard *that* one before."

"How about the one about people wearing their heart on their sleeve? That's you right now."

Will pulled a chair closer to the couch, sat down.

"I do have something I want to talk to you about," he said. "It's important."

"Told you," his dad said. "So what *is* so important to my boy?"

"I want you to coach our team," he said.

His dad didn't respond right away, just seemed to sink deeper into the couch, like he wanted it to swallow him up somehow. Closed his eyes, looking more tired than when he'd walked through the door. When he opened them, he turned his head and looked at Will and said, "Well, I certainly didn't see that coming."

"You're the best guy to do it," Will said. "The guys came up with a bunch of names. I kept running them through my head, all week long. But the name I kept coming back to was yours."

"This must have been Tim's idea, or Chris's or somebody's," Joe Tyler said. "Not yours. Because you know better. You have to know better."

"No, it was mine, Dad," Will said. "Even though I was the one who told the guys you couldn't, before somebody even asked."

"You're right. I can't."

"Yes, you can. Because, see, that's the thing; it's not that you can't. It's that you won't."

His dad carefully took the ice off his knee, set it on the coffee table, got into a sitting position, wincing again as he did.

In a quiet voice, like he was really curious, he said, "And why is that?"

It had only taken them this long to get down to it.

"You really want the truth?"

His dad said, "We just went over this. I'll know right away just by looking at you if it's not the truth. You know the real reason you're a bad liar? Because you never lie, at least not to me."

Will had his hands in his lap, wondering if Joe Tyler, who saw a lot even when you wondered if he was paying attention, could see now how hard Will was squeezing those hands together.

"I think you won't coach because you're afraid to coach," Will said. "Because you're afraid football might find a way to hurt you all over again. Because even though you watch football with me on television, and you watch my games, there's this part of you that hates football. And now if you won't coach the team, it'll be like you're taking it out on me."

"Afraid?"

Like he hadn't heard a word Will had said after that.

"Yeah, Dad, you are. Afraid of what football can do to you. When you're not just plain old mad."

"So if I turn you down, it *wouldn't* have anything to do with holding down one job and going to school in my spare time, which feels like another job? You don't suppose that it might have anything to do with *that*?"

He stepped on the last two words, his voice starting to rise up a little bit.

"And we haven't even discussed the job that's most important to me, which means trying to be the best father I can be for you. And mother. So maybe that's two more jobs."

Will said, "I know all you do, Dad."

"Do you? Well, of course you do, because it's clear you understand me *so* well."

Just like that, hearing the sarcasm in his dad's voice, Will felt something rising up in him. And his own voice along with it.

"You think I don't? You think I don't see how hard you work, and how much it hurts you? The way thinking about Mom does?"

Will saw the look on his dad's face as soon as he mentioned his mom, quickly added, "Sorry."

"No need. That's the truth, too."

"All I'm saying is, I get it, Dad. I'm not stupid."

He unclenched his hands.

"Didn't say that you were," his dad said.

"Like I said, I told the guys it was about work and school with you," Will said. "But I knew those weren't the real reasons. I knew they weren't the real reasons last year when I talked to you about being an assistant coach and you said no."

"So you think work and school are just some kind of cover story with me, is that it?"

"Yes," Will said in a soft voice. "But only as a way of getting out of coaching."

"That so?"

"I know you didn't give up playing football by choice, that you didn't want to give up something you loved that much," Will said. "But not ever coming back, that has been your choice."

Say it, Will told himself.

You've been giving this speech inside your head the last few days.

Say all of it.

"It was your choice to give up football forever," Will said, the words in a rush now to get out. "I know why you had to stop playing. But there's more to football than playing, and you know it. And you know—because I do—how much football you still have in you. I hear it every time we watch a game. I hear it every time you say something before the announcers do."

His dad leaned back into the couch.

"Why are we even talking about this?" his dad said, his voice the loudest it had been yet. "Even if I wanted to do it, I can't! There's no way we could come up with a decent practice schedule around my crazy schedule."

Will said, "I know your school schedule by heart. You go two nights one week, three the next. We could work around that easy. And practice on weekends if we had to, at least the one weekend day when we didn't have a game."

"Okay, let's say all of that is true. What about this? What about that I've never actually coached a team in my life, at any level? You guys are gonna want a real coach if you're gonna do this right. You're not doing this just to compete; I know you pretty good, too. You're doing this because you want to get back to the championship game and beat Castle Rock."

"I want you to coach," Will said.

His dad reached over, took a sip of lemonade, cleared his throat. Leaned back, looked at the ceiling, as if he might find the right words to say up there. He was still looking up when he said in a voice that was full of hurt, "I can't. As much as I try to love football watching you play, I've just hated it for too long. It took too much from me, kid. I've got you, and so I'd never say I've got some kind of crummy life. But apart from you, what's great about it up to here? Maybe after I get my degree, okay? But if we're keeping score on the life and times of Joe Tyler so far, it's not like I'm winning any trophies."

This was a story Will didn't know by heart, not like this.

His dad said, "I'm not saying I was going to the pros or anything like that; I wasn't *that* good. And even if I'd gotten a scholarship to a big school, that didn't mean I was going to beat out all the other recruits like me for a starting job. But after I got hurt . . ." He cleared his throat again. "After I got hurt, it was like I'd wrecked more than my knee, if that makes sense to you." He put his eyes back on his son now and said, "I'm still not sure I've come all the way back. Or if I ever will. So I get how much this matters to you. But football doesn't matter to me anymore. It hasn't since high school."

Will thought: *All in.*

"You're the one who's lying, Dad," Will said.

"Careful."

"You're the toughest guy I know," he said. "You *never* feel sorry for yourself, except when it comes to football."

"This conversation needs to be over."

"It's *true,* Dad. It is."

Like he was talking to Toby all over again, trying to get him to do more than listen, to really hear.

Will said, "You don't just have to do this for me, even though I want you to more than anything. You ought to do it for *you.* I remember everything you've ever told me about what it takes to be a good player, the way good players are supposed to act. But I've listened just as closely when you've told me about what it takes to be a good person."

Looking right at his dad, afraid to look away now.

"You're the one who says nobody goes through life unde-feated," Will said, his voice rising, surprising him. "You know we talk all the time about getting back up after you get knocked down. I just think that when it comes to football . . . well, it's time *you* got back up."

Then he was done.

So was Joe Tyler.

It took him two tries to get himself up off the couch; some-times that happened if he'd been off the knee for even a few minutes, it stiffened up on him that quickly. Sometimes he'd have to ask Will to give him a hand.

Not this time.

He stood up and Will was sure in that moment that he'd failed, that he'd taken this too far, crossed some kind of line that kids weren't supposed to cross with their parents.

At least he'd tried.

His dad turned and limped out of the room and a few seconds later Will heard the slow, painful walk up the stairs, Will some-times not sure whether it was the old stairs creaking or his dad.

Will didn't move.

Until.

Until he heard, "Will."

Got up and walked to the bottom of the stairs, and saw his dad at the top.

"You're right," he said.

"I'm . . . *right?*"

"I'll do it," Joe Tyler said.

Will stared up at him.

"I'll give it my best shot," he said. "Don't ask me to love it. I stopped loving football a long time ago, mostly because I found out it didn't love me back. So don't think that because I'm doing this, I'm gonna love it the way you do. I'm not sure anybody does. Okay?"

"Okay."

"But I'll do it."

Then he spread out his arms the way he did when he came home sometimes, when he was standing down where Will was now standing. Only Will Tyler wasn't there for long. In the next moment he was running up the stairs to where his dad was waiting for him.

He knew how bad his dad's knee was. But his arms felt stronger than ever.

12

His dad said he would get in touch with Mr. DeMartini's office first thing on Monday. Will was in charge of getting the nine other players they had so far to e-mail the size of their jerseys, pants, cleats, even hat sizes for the new helmets.

The two of them sitting there at the kitchen table.

"I've got to come up with a practice schedule that doesn't cheat you guys and works for me," Joe Tyler said.

Will grinned.

"Now, no missing assignments because of sports," Will said, wagging a finger at his dad.

"Not a problem," his dad said, serious again. "Those classes I'm taking are still my—*our*—ticket to a better life. I found out the hard way that it wasn't football."

Will said, "You're sure you want to do this."

His dad laughed. He didn't laugh a lot, but when he did, it was a good sound, at least to Will. A happy sound. That always made him wish he could hear more of it.

"Am I sure? Heck no!"

"I know I came at you pretty hard," Will said. "But you don't have to."

"Yeah," Joe Tyler said, "actually I do."

Then he asked Will what his best guess was on Toby, saying he thought it was important they have eleven players on the field for the first practice. Will told him the truth; going off his gut, he thought they had a real shot. But said at the same time he didn't want to put any more pressure on Toby than he already had; he was going to wait until school on Monday and then hope Toby would bring it up.

And then say yes.

"I remember that kid," Will's dad said. "Something about him I liked, even knowing he drew the worst-possible cards, getting Dick Keenan as an old man. But he could play. I'm not even positive what his best position is, as big as he is. We could sure use him."

The first time he'd said "we" when talking about the team.

Like they were officially in it together now.

"But we need more than him," his dad said. "We *both* know that. When I give them the sizes and order the uniforms this week, I'm gonna order one for him, just guessing his sizes. And then three more different sizes on top of that. Just being an optimist."

Will said, "I thought you were a pessimist."

"Don't press your luck, junior."

Some day, Will thought. And it wasn't over. Still a couple of hours before dinner.

"By the way, we're having hot dogs on the grill to celebrate," his dad said.

"What I'm talkin' about."

"Because you know what they say about hot dogs," Joe Tyler said.

They both knew the answer was one more inside joke between them, part of the secret language they shared, maybe because it had just been the two of them for so long.

"The hot dog," Will said, trying to sound like a deep commercial voice on television. "America's most underrated food group."

They high-fived each other.

Yeah, Will thought, *some day.*

Now he needed to run it off a little bit, blow off some steam. But in a good way. By himself. Run some sprints at Shea, just for the fun of it. And not totally for fun, because now he really was getting ready for a season.

He really did have to get in shape for football, not that Will Tyler was ever really out of shape.

He grabbed his ball from his room, told his dad he was heading for Shea, but that he'd be back in plenty of time for supper.

His dad by then was back on the couch, ice back on his knee, watching one of the first college football games of the season on television.

"Dad?"

"Yeah, bud."

"You're sure you're sure?"

"Go."

Then Will echoed what Toby had said to him a few hours ago and what already felt like something that had happened last week. "Thanks," he said.

His father's arm came up from the sofa, and then he jerked a thumb toward the front door.

"Go."

He thought about getting his bike out of the small garage, decided to walk to Shea instead.

After half a block, he started to jog.

By the time he got to Arch Street, ball under his arm, he was at full speed.

Football wasn't like basketball, where all you needed was a ball and a hoop to keep yourself entertained for as long as you wanted to be out there shooting around.

But even on a football field, even when he wasn't making up one of his imaginary games—and he wasn't doing that ever again, not if a girl might be watching—Will never had a problem keeping himself entertained.

Maybe because he was used to being alone. You had to put some effort into being alone. If you were going to do it, you might as well do it right.

So he ran his sprints, forty yarders at first, knowing that was the money distance in football, that's the one they were always timing at those NFL combines. He ran them with the ball at first and then without it. Took a breather. Ran a few more. He ran backward, knowing he was going to have to do some of that this season, that he was going to be dropping back in coverage as a free safety, that he probably wouldn't be off the field for a single play.

Then he went down near one of the goalposts and practiced his throwing, trying to hit one post, then the other, pretending they were skinny receivers. Doing that from ten yards, twenty, backing up to thirty, because he knew that was the limit for his arm. It was accurate; he could hit what he was aiming for. Definitely not a gun. Will knew that the way things were going, he might have to play some quarterback this season if there was nobody else, if only taking a direct snap in the wildcat.

He tried a few extra points, just goofing around—teams in their league only tried to kick extra points if they had a sure-footed kicker; most of the time they went for two from the two-and-a-half-yard line.

Finally, some punts. Because they might need a punter, too. Bobby Carrington, the quarterback who was leaving town, had handled the job last season. Bobby, in fact, had been such a good punter for an eleven-year-old that he'd turned punts into a weapon for them, occasionally burying their opponents inside the ten.

Now Bobby wasn't just taking his arm with him to Ohio; he was taking that big leg of his, too.

The next-best punter they had was Will.

Will stood out at the forty, trying to angle kicks out inside the ten the way Bobby had. He started with some gnarly-looking knucklers and wobblers, but then he got into it, got into rhythm, got off some good ones, the last one a dead spiral that looked like a pass he'd thrown high and deep, one that hit the sideline right at the five-yard line.

"One out of twenty?" he heard a voice say. "Is that a good percentage?"

Her.

Hannah.

Sitting in the first row of the bleachers, her ball next to her.

"You shouldn't sneak up on people," Will said. "And by the way? If you've been watching, you know that wasn't my only good kick."

Hannah said, "Yeah, it was. Put it this way: if this was a punt, pass and kick contest and you needed a kick to stay alive, well, you lose, Thrill."

"How do you know that's my nickname?"

"We go to the same school, remember?"

They were actually in three classes together and had been passing each other all week in the halls or seeing each other at lunch. Most of the time Will just nodded.

The most he'd said was, "Hey."

He had enough going on these days; he didn't need Tim LeBlanc or Chris or Jeremiah chirping at him because they thought he was giving the new girl the eye.

Even if that's exactly what he was doing.

Even if he secretly thought that Hannah Grayson, as cocky and obnoxious and annoying as she was, was a kickin' girl.

All ways.

Will grinned. "I've been trying to ignore that fact," he said. "And you."

"You sure about that?"

"Right," Will said, "that's how I spend my day now, checking you out."

"Well, not the whole day."

Smiling at him, like somehow she knew he'd been watching her make her way through her first week of school.

She stood up now and said, "Is this more fantasy football or would you like some company out there?"

"You mean you want to kick some?" he said.

"I want to play," Hannah Grayson said.

She picked up her ball and motioned toward the end zone where Will's ball had come to a rest, said to him, "Go long."

Will nodded and took off, getting up to full speed almost right away—he also had a *first* gear other guys didn't—and taking it right down the middle of the field, wanting more than anything to out-run the ball she was going to throw him, out-run her *arm*, be too far down the field for the ball to reach him.

"Ball!" she yelled as he crossed the twenty.

Will turned and looked up and saw the ball sailing over his head, landing at least ten yards ahead of him.

"I can see now you're not much of a kicker," Hannah said. "But I sort of *did* think you could run."

I got nothing, Will thought. *She airmailed me.* So he just picked up both balls, brought them back to midfield. "Seriously?" he said. "Are you always this full of yourself?"

"Why, 'cause I bust on you a little bit?" she said. "You know what my dad likes to say? Everybody thinks it's funny till it's about them."

"I give up," he said. "If this is a trash-talking competition, you win."

"Is it a competition?"

"Seems like it to me," Will said. "Or should I say, sounds like it?"

"Okay," she said, "I'll try to play nice."

They played.

Will passing to her, Hannah passing to him. They had kicking competitions, punting mostly. Hannah won easily. The girl could kick like a madman. Or madgirl. They had some running races. Will won. Will the Thrill *totally* thrilled that he'd beaten her, thinking he would have had to take his ball and go home if he hadn't.

Especially since she'd said this to him when they were taking their marks: "Listen, if I beat you, it will be our secret." Grinned and said, "Well, it will be between you and me and every other student at Forbes Middle."

"Keep chirping."

She held up a finger. One more thing. "And everybody who reads the *Dispatch.*"

"Not happening," Will said. "'Cause you're not beating me."

She didn't. But Will had to admit, she hadn't come up short in any of the other skill competitions. The girl was more than a kicker; Will had seen that with his own eyes now.

It killed him to admit this, too:

She was as good as she said she was.

Will knew it was getting close to dinner. He'd only come over here to work up a sweat and kill some time. But now he was in no hurry to leave, even though he knew he should.

One last thing he would *never* admit: he liked being with her. Here. Now.

It was when they took a rest finally, both of them stretched out in the grass in front of the bleachers, that she said, "I can play."

"I can see that."

"I mean," Hannah Grayson said, "I can play on your team."

"You want to play . . . on my team?"

"Is there an echo?" she said, whipping her head around.

"No, I'm just surprised is all. I mean, you kick like a champion . . ."

"Don't give me that, Mr. Thrill. You know I can do a lot more than that. I am, as guys like to say, a *playa*. And you need players, unless you've added a whole bunch since school ended on Friday. You're still sitting on ten and even a soccer girl knows you need eleven."

"But you *are* a soccer player."

"Bored with it. Been there, done that. But football with you guys? That would be a challenge. Big-time."

Now Will wanted to go home.

"Hey," he said, "even if I thought it was a good idea, which I'm not saying I do, my friends would never go for it. Neither would my coach."

"Thought you didn't have a coach."

"I'm wondering when you have time for school, being this much of a private detective."

She was smiling again. One more thing about her that made him feel like he was backing up. "Who's your coach? Maybe I should ask him myself."

"My dad. And don't bother. He's so old-school when it comes to football it's like he was around when they were building the school."

"Good one, Thrill. But how does he know he doesn't want me if he's never seen me play?"

Will said, "Why are we talking about this? You couldn't play on our team even if I . . . if *we* wanted you."

"Wrong," she said. "I looked it up. Nothing stopping me in the rules of the powerhouse West River league."

"You looked it up?"

"Went to the league's website. It's not rocket science. The rules say you have to be twelve, you have to have medical clearance to play, blah blah blah. Nothing that, uh, *discriminates* that I saw."

She turned *discriminates* into a hundred-yard word the way she dragged it out.

"I gotta get going soon," he said. "My dad is expecting me."

"Chicken."

"Because my dad's cooking dinner for us?"

"Because you're too chicken to ask your dorky friends about me or ask Coach Dad if he'll at least give me a tryout. And so you know? Any kid who wants to try out in a town is supposed to get the chance."

Will felt his shoulders drop, felt the air come out of him. "They would all think I've lost my mind."

"Does that mean you think I can't play? I thought you just told me I could."

"Hannah," he said.

First time he'd said her name out loud.

"It's *tackle football*," he said.

"You seem to have survived so far, little guy."

"I'm big enough."

"If you say so." Made a time-out sign with her hands. "I was just kidding with the last part. But you know you get by on speed and talent. So would I."

Will didn't know what to say. He did what felt natural to him. Stood up, picked up his ball. This girl had the ability to keep turning him around until he felt dizzy, almost. First he'd wanted to stay as long as he could with her. Now he wanted to get away as quickly as possible.

He knew he was the only one here acting flustered. She was just staring at him with this calm face.

"Before you go, just honestly answer one question for me," she said. "Do you, Will the Thrill, think I'm good enough to make the team?"

Even though it was just the two of them, nobody else in sight, Will gave a quick look around. "Yeah," he said. "I think you'd be good enough."

"So why can't I play on a team that needs players?"

"You're gonna make me come out and say it, right?" Will said.

She nodded.

"You can't play because you're a girl."

Now Hannah Grayson stood up, close to him, up in his space, maybe to show him she really was taller. Then she casually reached out and knocked his ball out of his hands.

As she walked away, she looked over her shoulder and said, "You're the girl."

13

They got together as a team for the first time the next Saturday afternoon at Shea.

No game jerseys yet, just the mesh practice jerseys New Balance had sent with the New Balance logo on the front, pads, pants, cleats. And helmets.

The boxes had arrived at the Tyler house on Friday, and the guys had all come by on Saturday morning to try stuff on. By the time they were in the living room, boxes ripped open, packing paper scattered everywhere, it reminded Will Tyler a little bit of Christmas morning.

Just bigger and louder and busier than any Christmas Will could remember. Most of the Christmases he'd ever experienced—not counting the one he'd spent in Florida with his mom's parents, his only living grandparents—had been him and his dad.

"So this is what new equipment feels like when you get to

take it home from the store," Tim said, his helmet already on his head. "Not just feels like, but *smells* like."

"I thought that was just your body wash," Will said.

Tim said, "You know, I've always heard there's a cruel side to great athletes."

Will put his own helmet on. "I just save it for you."

"Lucky me," Tim said.

"No," Chris Aiello said. "Lucky *us*."

They had passed the gear around, loving every minute of it, laughing and posing and even banging pads just for the fun of it. Like they really had found it under a tree.

When they were done, Will noticed that there were four extra sets, of everything.

When the guys were gone, Mr. Tyler having told them when to meet at Shea later, Will said to his dad, "Who's going to wear the extra gear, our ghost players?"

"Listen," his dad said, "the only one on this team with ghosts to worry about is me, and I'm gonna do my best to keep them under control. Or maybe get rid of them completely, if I'm the lucky one, by the end of the season."

"Be nice to fill out these uniforms," Will said. "Because we still can't field a team."

"How about we just do this today?" Joe Tyler said. "How about we just get on that field *as* a team and go from there?"

So now they were doing just that.

They were kneeling in one of the end zones in front of Will's dad, his dad wearing an old Forbes High School cap with a falcon on the front, gray sweatpants, an old Steelers sweatshirt.

And, Will noticed, not sure that any of the other guys did, his dad was also wearing an old pair of black, high-top Forbes Flyers football cleats.

With the wings.

Will didn't even know he still owned a pair. Didn't know *any-body* still owned a pair, in Forbes or anywhere else.

"Now Will knows this better than anyone," his dad was saying. "I'm not much for making speeches. Not much of a talker, period. When I do talk to you guys, I'm gonna try to do it without shouting, because when I was a player, I didn't want my coach shouting at me."

He moved slowly up and down in front of them as he spoke. No limp today.

"You guys don't need me to tell you how much we've overcome already, and how much we're going to have to overcome," he said. "Starting with the fact that we obviously need players. But one thing an old coach of mine did use to tell me was that you can only coach the players you have. So let's start there. Let's not worry today about what we *don't* have. Let's see what we *do* have. Okay?"

As if on cue the players in front of Joe Tyler said, "Okay!"

Shouting at the coach who said he wasn't going to, shouting like they meant it.

"In case anybody has any doubts, we are gonna play this season," he said. "And if that means lining up ten guys in our first game, then that's what we're gonna do. It may sound crazy, but I checked with the league and there's no rule written down that says we have to play eleven. In basketball, if you foul out a bunch of guys, you play with four."

Tim raised his hand. It was the first time Will could ever remember him asking for permission to speak.

"So we're going to let the rest of the league be on like a power play in hockey?"

"Until we get reinforcements."

"But what if we don't?" Will said. "Get reinforcements, I mean."

"If we don't, we're just gonna have to play bigger than we are. Which is what we're gonna have to do whether we get reinforcements or not. What we will do. To my way of thinking, it's still one of the best things about sports: you take a bunch of guys, different talents, egos, attitudes, different love for the game. And sometimes, if you really are lucky, they all get on the same page and do something greater than they ever thought they could."

He looked at every face in front of him now, one by one. Will. Tim. Chris. Jeremiah. Wes Blabey. Johnny Callahan. Gerry Dennis. Matt Connors. Ernie Accorsi. Jake Cantor.

"We're gonna be that kind of team," Joe Tyler said, "no matter how shorthanded we are."

He clapped his hands together.

"Okay," he said, "the meet and greet is over. We'll just do

some basic stuff today. Blocking fundamentals, tackling fundamentals. Got a couple of drills that won't be too boring. Then
we'll walk through some basic plays on offense, just to see what
we've got. And run some pass routes, see who's got enough arm
to be our quarterback, because Will told me about Bobby leaving town. So let's get to it. This team might not have the most
practice time in the world this season, but the time we do have
together, we're gonna make it count."

Watching his dad walk and talk and make his points and get
his message across, Will thought: *Not bad for a non-talker.*

"Oh, I almost forgot," Joe Tyler said, "one more thing before
we get to work, and I'm wide open to suggestions: what do we
call ourselves?"

Right away, guys were shouting out various nicknames.
Johnny Callahan actually did say, "Forbes Flyers!" But Chris came
right back at him, saying, "We may be shorthanded, but that
sounds too much like a hockey team." Jeremiah, a Yankees fan,
threw "Yankees" out there but got hooted down.

It went on this way for a few minutes, Giants being rejected
and Lions, for the Penn State Nittany Lions, until Will stood up,
grinning.

"Are we done here?" he said. "Because if we are, I've been
holding back the perfect name."

Now he was the one looking at his teammates, saying, "We
call ourselves the Bulldogs."

"Like the Georgia Bulldogs?" Tim said.

"Nope," he said. "The Forbes Bulldogs. We all know we're

going to be underdogs this season, probably in every game we play. I say we go with it. My dad has always talked about the toughest people being bulldog tough. That's us. Because who's gonna be tougher than us this season?"

"Nobody!" his teammates yelled, even louder than before.

One team, one voice.

"Then Bulldogs it is," Joe Tyler said. "Okay, you bad dogs. Let's get after it."

As they walked up the field, Will said to his dad, "I was worried you were going to tell us the one about how it's not the size of the dog in the fight, it's the size of the fight in the dog. That's always been one of your favorites."

"Decided not to overplay my hand," the coach of the Bulldogs said.

They practiced until it was almost too dark to keep going.

But the thing was? Nobody wanted to leave the field. Nobody wanted the first practice to end, ten guys on the field or not. Nobody seemed to get tired, even though Will's dad worked them pretty hard at times. Chris did the best in the passing drills, and when they were over, Joe Tyler said, "Boys, meet your new QB."

He said to Chris, "Can you handle it?"

"To be honest, Mr. T.?" Chris said. "I don't know if I can or not."

Will knew what was coming next.

His dad said, "If you don't think you can, you can't."

"Then I can," Chris said.

"What I'm talking about," Joe Tyler said. He grinned at the rest of them and said, "Hope all you guys pick up on my system that fast."

"Wait, you've got a system?" Tim said.

"Yes," Will's dad said. "And it often involves running laps during practice for players who don't know when to zip it."

Tim said, "Zippering it right now, Coach."

The best they could do was five-on-five, no running plays, passes only, but tackling allowed, Will's dad stressing that they were going to play clean, never leading with their fancy helmets. Yet when they had the chance to put somebody down, they should put them down hard.

"This is going to be a team of hitters," he said. "Quick hits on offense, hard hits on D."

On the last play of the night, it was just Chris and Will in the backfield, Chris snapping the ball to himself, three blockers in front of Chris, a simple swing pass to Will in the flat, what would be a screen pass when they were able to line up eleven.

Chris threw it to Will. Some daylight in front of him, but not much. Ernie and Jake were closest to him, but Tim was coming hard behind them along with Matt Connors, the fastest linebacker they had. Even in a game of five-on-five, this side of Shea had gotten very crowded all of a sudden.

But Will wasn't going to end their first practice with a no-gainer, whether they had the numbers on him or not. So as Tim closed on him, he planted his right foot and reversed his field. As he came the other way, running hard to his left now, he picked up Chris as a blocker, who laid out Matt.

Tim, not giving up on the play, seeing Will head to the left sideline, tried to get over there and cut down the angle, force him to the inside.

Will reversed his field again, but instead of running back to his right, he did take the inside, a sharp cut at full speed. Into that extra gear.

And then he knew he was gone and the guys on D knew he was gone and for that moment, even in what should have felt like a pickup game, a step up from the touch games they all played on this field, this felt like real football to Will, felt like the season was really starting.

Catch me if you can.

He knew no one could.

He ran through the end zone and right through the goalposts and as he did, he thought he saw somebody else running up ahead of him, into the woods behind the bleachers.

He wondered if it might be Hannah, watching again but not wanting to be seen.

Or maybe—and even better—Toby Keenan.

But Will wasn't going to chase after whoever it was, not after a run like he'd just made, after everybody had been chasing him. So he took one more hard turn and came back up the field to where his teammates were waiting for him. Practice officially over. His dad waving them into a circle, putting his hand out, the guys putting theirs on top of it.

"Bulldogs," Joe Tyler said.

"Bulldogs," they all said.

And then all you heard in the near darkness at Shea was this crazy barking from them, Will amazed that ten guys could make that much noise.

14

Hannah Grayson had taken to ignoring him at school. The one time he had tried to talk to her—after she'd called him a girl—was a jam-up, to say the least.

She had been avoiding even eye contact for the first three days of the school week, so on Thursday he just sat down next to her at lunch.

"That seat is taken," she said.

Will said, "Come on, you can't stay mad at me forever."

With that she just stood up and said, "Take this seat; it just opened up."

Will said, "Wait. How come this is all my fault?"

"Because it's your team."

"No, it's not."

"*Yes,*" she said, "it is. And if you don't know that, you're the only boy in the seventh grade who doesn't."

And then she was up and out of her chair in a blink, like she couldn't get away from him fast enough, nearly *running* away from him, head down. So she didn't see Tim LeBlanc and Jeremiah Keating walking across the middle of the room to bus their trays, Tim talking away as usual, neither one of them watching where they were going until the last second. Will almost yelled for her to watch out.

Then he saw that he didn't have to.

Hannah saw them at the last-possible second. As fast as she was moving, she made a sudden stop and spin move that Will would have been proud of on the football field, like she was avoiding a couple of tacklers who'd appeared out of nowhere.

Then she was out the door, untouched, and gone. Even Tim and Jeremiah stopped and watched her go.

Will sat there for a long time after she was gone, thinking about her, about the team, about how if Toby Keenan was going to change his mind, he would have done that already.

Mostly Will thought about how he still didn't have eleven players.

When his afternoon classes were over that day, he couldn't remember a single thing one of his teachers had said to him after lunch. Later, he couldn't remember anything Tim had said when they'd walked home.

He was stuck on something.

On some*body.*

His dad said, "A girl? You're joking, right? Tell me you're not serious."

"As a toothache."

"Good, because you're giving me one. Along with a head-ache." Joe Tyler pointed to Will, then at himself. "*You* want *me* to put a twelve-year-old girl on our team? On *your* team? No way."

This had been going on for a few minutes.

"You can't say that without at least giving her a look," Will said. "That's if I can get her to try out."

"*If?* If you can convince her? Were you playing without a hel-met before we got our new ones?"

This was Saturday morning. Their kitchen. Their usual Satur-day morning breakfast, pancakes and bacon. A tradition with them, like another part of their secret language, the bond be-tween them.

One being tested—severely—right now.

Will knew his dad wasn't done.

Joe Tyler said, "You're the one who says you don't want us to be a joke team. And now you want to put your new girlfriend on it?"

"She's not my girlfriend," Will said. "Right now, she's not even my friend."

"You want to know something? I don't care who she is. Or what kind of player you think she is. She's not going to be a player on any team of mine."

Will said, "It's not just yours."

"Good point! Excellent point, as a matter of fact! When we get to practice later, why don't you take a vote of the other guys on the team and ask them what kind of great idea they think this is. I'll help you count the votes."

Will knew that if he lost his cool, there was no way he'd get his dad to take a look at Hannah. Really see what she could do. And if he couldn't get his dad behind the idea, having his dad behind *him*, he had no way of selling it to Tim and Chris and the rest of the guys.

"Dad, do you think I'd even bring this up if I thought she *couldn't* play? I'm telling you, I've seen what she can do. And if you watched her catch and throw and run from a distance, you'd swear she was a guy."

"But she's not. And I wouldn't be watching her from a distance if I gave her a uniform. I'd be watching her from the sidelines. Afraid some big guy was gonna break her in two. It's why you gotta drop this. Now. And be happy you talked to me about it before you did your friends."

"No."

"No? Seriously?"

Will had waited until they'd finished eating. No reason to spoil a perfectly good pancake breakfast.

"First of all," his dad said, "the league will never go for it."

"She already looked it up on the website. There's no rule that says a girl can't play."

"Trust me on something, bud. Whatever the language is on their website, the league wouldn't want this even if I did. Which I don't."

Will said, "If she's good enough, she should have a chance. Isn't that what you've told me about sports my whole life? If you're good enough, somebody has to give you a chance."

That stopped his dad.

Who took a deep breath, let it out, made a motion with his hands like he wanted everybody to calm down here. Even though he'd been the only one getting worked up about the subject of Hannah Grayson joining the Bulldogs.

"Hear me out," Joe Tyler said. "Sometimes things aren't just about right or wrong. They're about the way things really *are*. And here's the way they are: it's a boys' league. Pop Warner was a boys' league before this one. And even if I thought this was worth doing, which I don't, you gotta be real, son. We've already got enough on our plate here. We don't need some controversy that's gonna end up on television and in the papers."

"She's not a controversy, Dad," Will said. "She's a good player. You could put her at wide receiver to keep her away from the action. And way back at safety. Let her punt and try extra points if you don't want her to run for them. You could hide her, Dad. But we'd have our eleven."

"Ten," his dad said. "We'd still have ten boys. And one girl. And as I said, how many of those other boys are gonna go along with this?"

"If I can get you to go along, I can get them to go along."

"You think they'll listen to you?"

"They usually do."

"Who's coaching this team, you or me?"

"Dad, you're the coach," Will said. "It doesn't mean I can't send in a play once in a while. Or a player."

His dad got up, walked over to the counter, refilled his coffee cup, sat back down.

"Just take a look at her," Will said. "That's all I'm asking. And if you really don't think she can help us, then I'll back down."

"But you're not gonna until I take a look at her, am I right?"

"*I'm* right," Will said.

His dad started to raise his coffee cup, put it back down, smiled.

"You want to know something amazing?"

"What?"

Joe Tyler said, "I had no idea you've been hanging on every word that came out of my mouth."

He reached over, speared the last piece of pancake on Will's plate, ate it, washed it down with coffee, stood up.

"Call Little Miss Sunshine and tell her to meet us at Shea in an hour," Will's dad said.

When Will did, Hannah wanted to know why she had to try out.

"Did anybody else have to?" she said.

Will said, "Can you do me one favor today? Try to be nice."

"Nice doesn't have anything to do with it," she said. "It's not like I was begging for a chance to come play with you losers."

Will almost hung up right there. But he didn't. He should have known she'd be a harder sell than his dad.

"You're the one who said you wanted to play," Will said. "Do you want to play or not?"

Now there was a long pause at her end. Will was half-waiting to hear the dial tone that would have meant she'd hung up on him first.

"I want to play."

"That's what I thought. And Hannah?"

Will didn't know why he liked saying her name, hearing the sound of it as it came out of his mouth. But he did.

"What?"

"By nice I mean, please don't talk to my dad in the mean way you talk to me," Will said, then added, "See you at the field."

Then hung up before she *could* be mean.

But she was totally different with Will's dad, like a completely different girl from the moment Will introduced them.

"Very nice to meet you, Mr. Tyler. Will's told me so much about you."

(Will thinking: *When exactly did we have* that *conversation?*)

"I couldn't believe it when he told me you'd agreed to coach the team!"

(*Or that one.*)

"Anyway," she said, "thanks so much for giving some crazy girl you don't even know a chance to try out for you, on a day when you have practice later."

(Will thinking: *Well, at least the crazy part is true.*)

When she was done blowing smoke at him, Will's dad said, "Now that we've got the introductions out of the way, I need to ask you a serious question, Hannah: why do you want to do this, for real?"

Hannah Grayson had her hair in a ponytail today, was wearing shorts and a blue Michigan T-shirt with a yellow *M* on the front. And cleats. They were soccer cleats, but she clearly wasn't messing around.

As usual, she had brought her own ball.

She took a moment to answer.

"Because," she said. "I've got something to prove."

"*What* do you have to prove?"

"That I'm as good as they are," she said.

Nodding at Will. Nodding at one boy like he was all the boys.

Joe Tyler stared at her now, like he was taking another look at the tall girl with the ponytail, football under her arm. Probably seeing for the first time what Will had seen the first day, that this girl didn't back up very much, either.

"Well, then, let's see what you got," Will's dad said. "Because it seems to me that just about everybody on this team has something to prove."

Joe Tyler didn't go easy on her, or Will, working them both out, as if Will had come here to try out the same as Hannah had. Will had thought his dad would have her do some punting and placekicking first, just to see if she had as much leg as Will said she did.

But he didn't. He made them run first, made them run a *lot*, made them run a forty, take a break, then run another one. Will was still beating her the way he had when they'd raced on this field before. But not by a lot. Not the way he could beat Tim or Chris or Johnny Callahan, the next-fastest guy on the Bulldogs.

Joe Tyler made Hannah cover Will on pass routes, then had Will cover her. Then he had Will punt some to her, just to see how she did holding on to a ball coming down at her out of the sky. One time Joe Tyler surprised her while the ball was still in the air, coming at her in that slow, wobbly run of his, just to dial up the pressure a little bit, see if she could handle the pressure *and* the ball.

She did.

Not only caught the ball, but then gave the creaky old guy in front of her a sweet head fake, faking him out so badly he nearly fell down, blowing past him, running at full speed the whole length of the field.

Taking it to the house.

When she got to the far end zone, she turned around, put the ball on her hip. If Will knew anything about this girl by now, he knew she wanted to say something in that moment. But she didn't. She wasn't here to trash-talk Will or even win him over; she already had that victory just by being here. Hannah was here to impress Will's dad. Win *him* over. Like she was trying to show a new teacher that she was the brightest kid in class.

And for now, the best way to do that was to keep her mouth shut. Will thought of a line he'd read from Buck Showalter, the Orioles manager, telling one of his players one time, "I can't hear a word you're saying because your actions are shouting too loudly at me."

That was Hannah today.

Joe Tyler didn't say anything, just motioned her up to mid-field, saying, "We're not done, you know?"

"Just getting warmed up, Coach," she said.

They weren't in pads, Will wondering if she even had pads, if any girl anywhere had pads. So there was no contact of any kind. Both Will and Hannah ran a few more pass routes, Joe Tyler doing the throwing this time, and then finally it was time for Hannah to do some kicking.

She started with punting and it was here, where Will least expected it, that the mouthy, cocky girl showed some nerves, shanking the first one. But after that she got into it, kicked about six beauties in a row, even angling them inside the ten-yard line when Will's dad asked her to try that.

Finally, placekicking. Just simple extra points, Joe Tyler doing the snapping as if he'd been a long snapper his whole life, Will holding for Hannah, even spinning the ball like a pro so that the laces faced away from her.

She made ten kicks in a row and they were done.

"You're as good as Will said," Joe Tyler said. "So we're gonna give this a shot."

Hannah smiled, one of her big ones. "Thank you," she said. "And just so you know, I'm not afraid of getting hit. If I was, I wouldn't have tried out."

"You may not be afraid," Will's dad said. "But I am. Not every-body in this league is my son's size."

"Hey," Will said.

Grinning as he did.

"And there are going to be some jerks who are going to want to put it to you just to show how tough they are, or show you how much they don't want a girl playing *their* game. Like it makes them feel less like guys somehow. So they'll be looking to, I don't know . . ."

"Compensate?" Hannah said.

"Exactly. Smart girl."

"Smarter than most boys," she said.

Unable to help herself.

"Most girls are," Will's dad said.

"Hey," Will said again.

"Facts are facts, son." To Hannah, Joe Tyler said, "I'll need to talk to your parents. I assume this is all right with them, or you wouldn't be here."

"My dad a lot more than my mom," Hannah said. "You'll see when you talk to them. But they said if I wanted to do this, they wouldn't stand in my way."

Will's dad shook his head.

"I may be crazy," he said. "No, check that. I *am* crazy or I wouldn't be here myself. But we started this day with ten play-ers and now we've got one more, as far as I'm concerned."

"Cool," Hannah said.

"But there's one thing: we gotta get the other guys on board with this."

"Wait a second, Mr. Tyler," Hannah said. Like she was digging in. *"You're* the coach. And there'd be no team without *him."*

Nodding at Will again.

"You're right, there'd be no team without Will," Joe Tyler said. "But on every good team I was ever around, it was all for one."

He shrugged at Hannah, smiled.

"Now we gotta see how that theory holds up when you're the one," Will's dad said.

15

Convincing his dad about Hannah turned out to be a piece of cake compared to convincing his teammates.

The most vocal of them, surprising Will, was Tim LeBlanc.

Not surprising Will by being the most vocal—that was a given with his best friend. The only time he would shut up was when a teacher would threaten him with a lunch detention.

No. The surprise here was just how much Tim, the closest thing Will had to a brother, was dead-solid set against the idea of putting Hannah on the team.

"Why don't we just change our name to the Poodles?" he said.

Everything he was saying before practice was directed at Will. Not Will's dad, the coach of the team.

Just Will.

"That's not funny," Will said.

"For once, I'm not trying to be funny," Tim said.

Will tried to be, just wanting to chill him out a little. "It must be a struggle," he said.

"No," Tim said. "But what *is* a struggle for the rest of us is look-ing at a whole season of being the butt end of jokes because you came up with the genius idea of us adding a girl to the roster."

"She can help us," Will said. "Do you really think I'd do some-thing, after we've gotten this far, to *hurt* us?"

Tim ignored the question. "I thought this was supposed to be the West River league," he said. "Not *A League of Their Own*."

It was a movie they'd watched one time about a women's professional baseball league. The one where the manager said there was no crying in baseball.

"You haven't seen her yet," Will said, "but you've already made up your mind. That's not right."

"What's not *right* is her jamming up the rest of us and making us look pathetic," Tim said.

They were in a circle at midfield. Every time Tim stopped talk-ing, the rest of the Bulldogs were staring right at Will.

Now he went at them.

"What do the rest of you guys have to say?" Will said. "LeBlanc may be the loudest voice on the team, but it's not the only one."

Chris said, "I didn't sign on to play with girls."

Jeremiah said, "Same."

"Same," Wes said.

"It's not a bunch of girls," Will said. "It's one girl."

"All it takes," Chris said.

"One girl who seems to be, like, dominating you," Tim said.

"Are you joking?" Will said. "She wasn't even speaking to me until today."

"But I'll bet she was fine as soon as you gave her what she wanted," Tim said. "Just flat-out promised her a spot on the team before you even talked to the rest of us. *Sweet.*"

"If I'd promised her a spot," Will said, "we wouldn't be having this conversation."

Thinking: he and Tim had never seriously fought about anything, until now. Fighting over a girl. Just not the way guys usually did.

"The only thing I promise," Will said, "is that she can help us."

Johnny Callahan said, "In what? A flag football league?"

Will said, "Dude, I hear you. Hannah knows this better than anybody: the first time she told me she wanted to play on our team, I shot her down big-time. She wouldn't even talk to me." He shrugged. "But I'm telling you, I was wrong about her."

"Why?" Tim said. "Because she's talking to you again?"

"You know how much I want to win," Will said. "In everything. You know I wouldn't be doing this if I didn't think she could help us win."

He looked over at his dad now, the look basically saying this: Jump in anytime.

He did, just not the way Will expected.

"I agree with the guys," Joe Tyler said.

Will stared at his dad, trying to keep his face calm, hoping the other guys couldn't *hear* all the air coming out of him the way it did when you popped a balloon.

"When I was your age, I would've quit before I lined up with a girl," he said. "Are you kidding? In this town in the old days, when we thought we were the toughest guys around? They wouldn't have just wanted to change our name to the Poodles; guys from other towns would have been asking us why we weren't playing in *skirts.*"

He put his hands up, like surrendering.

"I told Will we'd put this to a vote, and we don't even have to do that; I'm feelin' you guys on this," Joe Tyler said. "So the best thing is to call the whole thing off now. You can drop your equipment off at the house in the morning. I'll call the league. Will should probably be the one to call New Balance."

Tim hadn't seen *that* coming.

"Wait a second, Mr. T.!" he said. "Nobody said anything about the rest of us quitting. We just don't want a girl on the team."

"But you see, that's a problem, Timmy. Not for you, but for me. Even though I told Hannah that we'd have to hear from the rest of you guys, I frankly didn't expect this kind of reaction. So she left my house feeling as if she was on the team. And I let her think that. As far as I'm concerned, that's the same as if I gave her my word. The same as when I gave Will my word that I'd coach the team. Once I do that, I never go back."

"But, Coach," Chris said, "*you* just said that you would've quit rather than play with a girl when you were our age."

Joe Tyler smiled now, at Chris, at all of them.

"Yeah, son, I did. But that's only because I was a whole lot dumber at your age than I am now. About almost everything."

"Not wanting to play with a girl doesn't make us dumb," Tim said.

"Didn't say it did," Will's dad said. "It just makes you a guy. And now I want you to listen to this guy." Poking a finger at his own chest. Backing up, so he was talking to all of them at once.

Now he was pointing to his left shoulder.

"Whether you can see it or not," he said, "there's a chip on that shoulder. It's there tonight, it's gonna be there for our first game, it's gonna be there all season. There's a chip on my shoulder, and Will's, and Tim's. Everybody's on this team."

His voice was rising. He had their attention now. Will's, too. Looking at his dad and maybe seeing him as his coach for the first time.

"And this girl, whether you want her with us or not, has that same kind of chip. She doesn't just want to show other teams. She knows she's gonna have to show her *own* team. She wants to help us show everybody that a team from a nowhere town like this—and you know that's what other people think about Forbes now—can take on anybody."

Joe Tyler was out of breath, the way he was sometimes just climbing up the stairs.

"So I'm gonna ask something now," he said. "I'll ask Timmy first. You with me?"

There was just a slight hesitation, then Tim LeBlanc looked up at Will's dad, nodded.

"I'm with you, Coach," he said.

"Chris?"

Chris Aiello had been kneeling. Now he stood up.

"With you," he said.

The rest of the Bulldogs stood up.

"I think we're all with you," Will said.

Then Will saw his dad looking past them, toward the arch, Hannah Grayson walking through it, ball under her arm, what must have been her own helmet on her head, shoulder pads showing under the oversized sweatshirt she was wearing as a practice jersey.

As she got closer to them, Will could see the number she'd obviously drawn on the front of the sweatshirt herself.

11.

Will had to admit:

As cocky as she was, the girl did have style.

"Yeah," Joe Tyler said, pointing to his own shoulder again. "Here comes a girl with a chip on hers."

16

"A wkward," Tim said loud enough for only Will to hear.

Will said, "Just pretend she's one more person hanging on every word you say."

"What do you mean *pretend*?"

But it was awkward at first, the guys introducing themselves by their first names one by one, even though they all went to the same school with Hannah Grayson.

Hannah was still on her best behavior, taking a minute to tell them she understood how this was probably weirding them all out but that she was sure she could help the team and, besides, it wasn't like she was taking somebody else's position.

Then she said to the rest of the Bulldogs what she had said to Will.

"I *can* play," she said. "I know I'll have to prove it at every practice and at every game. But I can play."

Tim said, "That all looks like new equipment. You sure you're not gonna mind getting it dirty?"

Testing her right away.

Hannah gave him her best smile.

"Watch me," she said.

A lot of the night's practice was putting all eleven of them in their offensive positions, walking them through the plays that Will's dad had put in already, then running them at full speed through the orange cones that Joe Tyler had set up as ghost defenders. Trying to give them a general sense, he said, of where the defense would be when they tried to run these plays in a real game. Against real players.

Will couldn't tell whether his dad really wanted to school them on the plays or whether he was purposely avoiding any contact drills, not wanting Hannah to get flattened at her first practice.

Joe Tyler just kept lining her up at wide receiver. Chris Aiello finally threw her way on the third pass play of the night, a simple sideline pattern.

Ball went right through her hands.

"Great," Tim said, standing next to Will in the backfield. "Girl's got hands like feet."

"Shut it."

"Truth hurt?"

"You know that all-for-one thing my dad always talks about?" Will said. "I'm pretty sure it's supposed to last longer than one series of downs."

Joe Tyler's only reaction to the drop was to say, "Run it again."

When Hannah took her position, Will's dad said, "This time hold on to it."

It was the kind of thing he said to the rest of them when they messed up.

They ran it again. Chris's throw was high this time. Hannah Grayson reached up, made a terrific hands catch, even managed to keep both feet inbounds as she did.

"Better," Will's dad said.

They had been at it for two hours, Shea getting dark now, when Joe Tyler said, "Okay, let's scrimmage for a few minutes. Like we do. Five on offense tonight, six on defense. Chris can snap it to himself. Two guys in front of him, Hannah and Johnny at wide receiver. Empty backfield. Ball on the twenty. Pretend like it's overtime in college football and the offense wins if it scores a TD, defense wins if it gets a stop."

Tim was the one who asked the question.

"Full contact?" he said.

"Tackle football, boys," Joe Tyler said. "And girl."

Wes and Gerry Dennis rushed the quarterback. Ernie Accorsi was the one linebacker; Jake Cantor said he'd roam as free safety. That left Will and Tim as the cover guys.

"I'll take her," Tim said.

"No," Will said. "I will."

"So you can go easy on her?"

"Do I ever go easy on you, big boy?"

Tim said, "If she catches it and you get the chance to put her down, you're saying you will?"

"Hundred percent."

Will wishing he was as sure of that as he sounded.

Hoping that Chris kept throwing to the other side of the field.

But Chris missed Johnny on first down. Overthrew him badly on second. Rolled out and got tackled for no gain by Ernie on third down.

Fourth-and-ten.

It was right here, right now, that the jock in Will kicked in. He didn't want them to score. He wanted the defense to win, even in a five-on-six scrimmage, and the field was getting darker by the minute.

"Let's switch," Will said to Tim. "I'll take Johnny."

"You think I can't cover him?"

Will grinned. "No," he said. "But I *know* I can."

As Tim walked away, Will could hear him saying, "Please throw it to her. Please, please, *please.*"

Will said, "You really are an idiot."

"Please," Tim said.

Tim LeBlanc got his wish.

And promptly got beat.

By a girl.

He must have been sure that if Chris did throw it her way, it would be another sideline pass; it's all they'd been throwing her way in the walk-through, then the run-through.

Will saw it all happen from the other side of the field once he saw Chris Aiello looking Hannah's way. If there was one thing Will had picked up on already, it was that Chris—new to the position—never looked off a receiver. Once his eyes locked on somebody, the ball was going his way.

Or hers.

Will saw Hannah plant her right foot like she was cutting to the sideline. As she did, he saw Tim move around her to the outside, where he was sure the ball was coming, Will knowing his bud like he knew his name, knowing he wanted to end the scrimmage with a pick.

But as soon as Hannah felt him on her outside shoulder, she planted her *outside* foot, crossing him up, crossing to the middle of the field on a simple post pattern.

Dusting Tim in the process.

He scrambled to catch up with her but was a good five yards behind.

Chris threw a tight spiral this time, leading her perfectly, his best pass of the night. Ernie was out of position, Jake had been shading toward Johnny Callahan, the middle of the field was wide open.

Nothing but green.

Her only mistake was breaking stride as she caught the ball, being careful to lock the ball into her arms, as if she wanted to make sure she didn't drop it.

It gave Will a couple of extra steps to get over there. The only question now, because Hannah had slowed down just enough, was whether Will or Tim was going to get to her first.

Will made sure it was him. He was faster than Tim now, the

way he always was, and he figured that even his hardest hit wasn't going to be as hard as Tim's, especially not after she had just faked him out of his new cleats.

Low or high?

Easy decision; Will wasn't going to take a chance coming in high, even against a girl; he had this way of bouncing off *all* ball carriers when he tried to hit them high. The safest and surest tackle was to come in hard and low, wrap her up with his arms and bring her down, well short of the goal line.

It's exactly what he did. A good, hard, clean hit that did the job, just short of the ten-yard line. Scrimmage over. The defense had won.

Will got up first. But Hannah Grayson wasn't far behind him, popping up like she was bouncing on a trampoline. Right up in his face.

"What do you think you're doing?" she yelled.

She was about to give him a shove, Will was sure of it. He could see her eyes through her face mask, see how hot she was. But Hannah stopped herself at the last second, pulled her hand down, Will happy about that, at least, not sure what he would have done in front of the guys if she *had* knocked him back.

"What am I *doing*?" he said. "Tackling you, that's what I'm doing."

Hannah yanked her chin strap, pulled off her helmet. "You think I'm mad that you *tackled* me? Are you in*sane*?"

Will said, "Then what *are* you so mad about?"

Hannah said, "If you're gonna hit me, do it like you mean it."

Then she walked away.

Will stood where he was, glad she hadn't waited for an answer, embarrassed to tell her or the rest of the guys that he thought he *had* hit her like he meant it.

17

The uniforms were as close as they could get to the color of the throwback jerseys the Steelers wore a couple of times a year, somewhere between red and brown.

"Rust," Will's dad said. "Like the rust on me."

The Riddell helmets were as plain as they could be, as plain as his dad's other favorite football team, Penn State, no numbers, no logos, just a simple stripe the color of the jerseys.

The people at New Balance, once they had the sizes, somehow outfitted the Bulldogs at what seemed like world record speed to Will. His dad said that money had a way of speeding up any process.

But he was happy when he opened the first box, because he had designed the look he wanted for the Bulldogs himself. Throwback jerseys, old-school helmets.

"It's just the way I see us," Joe Tyler said. "Bulldogs, just without the bull."

Will grinned. "That leaves us with dogs," he said. "Heavy on the under."

The uniforms showed up on Thursday before their first game. By then, Hannah Grayson was an official member of the team, about to wear the same number 11 she'd worn to her first practice. The other coaches in the West River league didn't like the idea of a girl playing; Will could tell that the night his dad was on a conference call with them, just listening from the top of the stairs to his dad's end of the conversation.

But Joe Tyler finally—and calmly—wore them down, making it sound as if Hannah and her parents were prepared to sue if the league refused to let her play.

He had also let them know that if he had to hang up and tell the Graysons that their daughter wouldn't be playing against Palmer on Saturday, they could all expect to be attacked by the Forbes *Dispatch* and the other papers in Mr. Grayson's chain. And once that happened, they shouldn't be surprised to see the story picked up on television.

Will heard his dad say, "You know what they say about newspapers. Never pick a fight with somebody who buys ink by the barrel."

When his dad finally finished up, Will said, "Where'd you get the one about ink by the barrel?"

"Mark Twain. He was my favorite writer even before I went back to school."

Will said, "And the part about the Graysons suing? I don't remember Hannah ever mentioning that to me."

"Well, I never actually *said* they were going to sue," his dad said. "Just call it a good ball fake."

"But not a lie. Because that would be wrong wrong wrong."

"This is football," his dad said. "You never heard of a little misdirection?"

So they had a full team. On Saturday they were going to start the season, ready or not.

Not, as it turned out.

Palmer was about a half hour east of Forbes. But even though it was smaller than Forbes, its high school team was always one of the best in the area, and so were its town teams.

Last year, Will's team had lost just twice during the regular season, one to Castle Rock, one to Palmer, Palmer beating them on a long touchdown pass in the last minute, thrown by a kid named Ryan Webb, who had the second-best arm in the league after Castle Rock's Ben Clark.

Ryan was still on the team, Will saw that during warm-ups, looking bigger than ever, as if he'd started growing at the end of last season and still hadn't stopped.

"Is that a twelve-year-old like us," Tim said, "or Cam Newton?"

"He does look like he's got a shot at the Heisman, doesn't he?" Will said.

It didn't take long for Will to find out that Ryan Webb and his teammates knew about Hannah being on their team.

Ryan had caught Will's eye from his end of the field, motioned for them to meet up at midfield, Will thinking that one thing never seemed to change in sports, the best guys always felt as if they knew each other better than they actually did. Like they were in the same club, even though they were on different teams.

Ryan really did remind Will of Cam Newton, not just his face but his body, the biggest kid on the Palmer team playing quarterback. When he took off his helmet, Will noticed he was wearing the same kind of thick orange headband that Cam Newton wore under *his* helmet.

They shook hands and then Ryan nodded past Will to where the rest of the Bulldogs were stretching.

"The rest of your team coming on another bus?" he said.

"No, this is all of us," Will said. "But I'm pretty sure you can only line up eleven at a time."

"I heard that's all you had, but I still thought you'd've added at least a couple more."

Will shook his head.

"And it's for real you brought a girl?"

Now Will nodded.

Ryan said, "You guys are gonna play with a *chick*?"

"Better not let her hear you call her that."

"Why?" Ryan Webb said, smiling. "She gonna post a mean message about me on her Facebook page?"

"Hey," Will said, "she might surprise you."

Wondering if he was going to spend the whole season having conversations like this.

"Surprise me how?" Ryan said. "Going the whole game without crying?"

Will reached up then, lightly banged on Ryan's shoulder pads, said, "Have a good one, dude," and jogged back to where Tim and Chris were waiting for him.

"What was that all about?" Tim said.

"What do you think?"

"Your daddy's little girl?"

"Pretty much."

Hannah was standing at the forty now, standing next to Will's dad, getting off one good punt after another to Johnny Callahan.

Please, Will thought.

Please let her at least kick well today.

A few minutes before the kick, Joe Tyler called the players in around him.

"This is just a beginning today," he said. "But it's a beginning that I have a feeling means more to us than it does to them." He looked down the field at the Palmer Wildcats. "They've got more players than us, probably have had more practice time. Looks to me like they can practice eleven-on-eleven. We don't have that luxury. Heck, the only luxury for us is the uniforms you're wearing. And I don't care about any of it."

Looking around at the faces looking at him.

"We've got talent, we've got heart." Pointed to his shoulder. "And we've got that chip."

Joe Tyler put his hand out. They all put theirs on top. Somehow Will never got tired of doing it.

"Whatever happens in this game, we're gonna be better at the end of it than we are right now."

He looked at Will now.

"And if we get knocked down today, we get back up, and we keep coming, no matter what."

"One, two, three, dogs," he said.

They yelled back at him in one loud voice.

They won the coin toss and elected to receive; Will returned the opening kickoff to the Bulldogs' thirty-five-yard line. Then he gained four yards on each of his first two carries, Will feeling as if he'd earned every inch of the eight yards that brought them to third-and-two.

Chris looked over to Will's dad for the play.

"Thirty-four lead," Chris said in the huddle.

It took Tim out of the slot and put him in the backfield as a fullback. Chris would fake the ball to him, then give it to Will, who would follow Tim through what was supposed to be a great big hole between right guard and right tackle.

Tim sold the fake about as well as you could and headed through the hole ahead of Will, right at the middle linebacker. His mission: knock him down or at least slow him down enough for Will to run past, find some open field.

The ball was in Will's hands now. Wes and Jeremiah had done their job getting off the ball and holding their blocks, Will waiting to see once he'd cleared them whether he should keep running up the middle, where Tim would be trying to cut down the middle linebacker, or cut to the outside. From the time Will had first started playing, his dad had told him that you had to wait for your blocks to develop.

The best opening was inside.

Will wasn't thinking about just making the first down now; he knew there was a chance for a big play. *Feeling* the play, one his dad said went all the way back to his days at Forbes High, Will past the line of scrimmage now, not sure where Ryan Webb was but already looking to see where the safeties were.

Worrying about that when he was still in some traffic, not protecting the ball the way he should have. Not seeing the cornerback coming from his right side, swinging his arm the way they were all taught now, punching it perfectly out from under Will's arm and into the air.

On the third play from scrimmage.

Out from under Will's arm and into the hands of Ryan Webb. Like a power forward standing under the basket and having a rebound just fall into his hands.

Will's momentum was still going forward. Ryan Webb, having made his thank-you-very-much fumble recovery, was already running the other way.

Will got himself turned around, tried to get himself back in the play. But the last Bulldog to have a chance to stop him or even slow him down was Hannah Grayson, chasing Ryan from his right, trying to get an angle on him.

Ryan could have cut away from her easily, toward the goal line pylon to his left.

Instead he slowed down, waited for Hannah to get right up on him, then straight-armed her as hard as he could, dropping her at the fifteen-yard line.

Ryan scored easily, never looking back. The Wildcats went for a two-point conversion, made it. Just like that it was 8–0, Palmer. Will had waited since last season to make up for the fumble that had lost the championship game and now he had fumbled the third time he touched the ball this season.

The Bulldogs got the ball back, went three and out. Hannah hit a pretty good punt, but it didn't matter, because on first down Ryan Webb threw one as far as he could and one of his wide receivers caught it, and even though the Wildcats missed the conversion, this time they were already ahead 14–0.

A few plays later Chris tried to throw one over the middle to Johnny Callahan, but one of the safeties jumped the route and took it the other way for a pick-six score. Ryan Webb faked a handoff and bootlegged his way to another two-point conversion, untouched.

It was 22–0, Palmer. And would get worse after that, the Bulldogs going three and out, and Palmer grinding out the last five minutes of the half and scoring again. They failed on the two-point conversion. Small consolation.

Palmer led 28–0. At halftime.

As Will ran to his sideline, Ryan ran up alongside him.

"Yo, Tyler," he said. "You guys are aware this game *counts*, right?"

Then he added this:

"You sure you only got *one* girl on the team?"

No one on the Bulldogs quit.

Halfway through the third quarter Will ran up on a short punt, got a great block from Chris Aiello and another one from Hannah down the field, ended up going fifty-five yards for the Bulldogs' first score of the season.

Hannah kicked the point as if she'd been doing it for boys' teams her whole life and it was 28–7.

But then Palmer went on a long ten-play drive, mostly running it now the Bulldogs getting tired on defense, just plain worn down. Ryan Webb finally scored on a quarterback draw from the ten-yard line. Then he threw for the two-point conversion to a wide-open tight end in the back of the end zone.

Now it was 36–7, with three minutes left.

Before the kickoff, Joe Tyler grabbed Will and said, "The guys are gonna look at you more than ever right now. Act like this is the biggest drive of the whole year."

"Dad, we're getting killed whether we score or not." - -

Joe Tyler put his hands on Will's shoulders and said, "Never let anyone see you give up. If it helps, just think of it this way: even one more drive working against a real defense will help us next week."

Will busted the kick return all the way to the forty. When he got into the huddle, he said, "Let's show 'em what we've got."

Tim, hands on knees, clearly tired, said, "Can't we just show 'em what we *don't*?"

"They're gonna want to stick it to us with one more stop,"

Will said. "We might play these guys again. Let's stick it to *them* with one more score."

Trying to act pumped up, as if it were the Steelers going down the field to win the Super Bowl against the Cardinals back in 2009.

On second down they ran a regular 38 Toss. Jeremiah threw a great block on the defensive end, Johnny Callahan cleaned out the corner covering him and Will ran all the way to the Palmer twenty-two before getting knocked out-of-bounds.

Two minutes left.

Will telling himself he would have given anything a few weeks ago to have two minutes to score, even in a losing game.

Chris overthrew Johnny on first down. Second-and-ten. As they were waiting for Johnny to get back to the huddle, Chris looked over to Joe Tyler, told everybody else in the huddle they were supposed to run the same play all over again.

Will said, "Throw it to Hannah instead. We haven't thrown to her once all day."

"I thought the quarterback got to call the audibles," Chris said.

Will said, "I'm not changing the play, just the receiver."

The play was simple enough: Go-7-Go. Both wideouts, Johnny and Hannah, just took off on the snap and ran straight down their sidelines. Tim, the underneath guy, looked as if he were doing the same thing down the middle of the field, then stopped and came back on a buttonhook.

In the huddle Chris told Tim to keep going and Hannah to come back for a buttonhook near the sideline.

Tim looked at Will, who said, "They won't be expecting it."

Hannah just nodded.

Will stayed home to block for Chris, picked up a blitzing line-backer, giving his quarterback enough time to throw. He had a great view of the play, Hannah faking out the corner covering her, getting herself open at the first-down marker, Chris making one of his better throws of the day.

Knowing they were out of time-outs and knowing she had the first down, Hannah looked the ball into her hands, then just looked to step out-of-bounds.

Before she did, the cornerback covering her, coming back to her and the play at full speed, just buried her, even though everybody watching the play knew she was going out-of-bounds.

Nothing illegal about the hit; she was still inbounds. But a total cheap shot as far as Will was concerned. He was already heading over there before Hannah went skidding toward the Bulldogs' bench. But his dad had a shorter distance to cover, even on his creaky leg. Before he leaned down to see if Hannah was all right, he turned and put out his hand to Will and the rest of the Bulldogs, telling them to stay where they were.

"Stay!" he yelled.

Not sure if they were running for Hannah or the cornerback, not wanting any trouble, any kind of fight, when the fight was really over today.

Joe Tyler put a hand down to help Hannah up, but she ignored it, pulling herself up on her own. Like the whole thing was no big deal. Will watched her tip her helmet back, take out her mouthpiece, say something to Will's dad. Saw his dad smile and put an arm around her.

Will would ask his dad later what Hannah had said.

"She wanted to know if we should throw again on third-and-ten or try to fool them with a run," Joe Tyler said.

When she got back to the huddle, she had brought the next play with her.

"Sweep 7," she said.

"You sure you're okay?" Will said.

"Do I ask you if you're okay every time you get tackled?" she said.

The play was a simple pitch to Will on a sweep left, which meant Hannah's side of the field. It would give her a chance to block the cornerback who had just clobbered her.

Only Hannah never got a chance to throw her block.

Somehow Tim, showing as much speed as Will had ever seen from him, got to the corner first. Ernie Accorsi, playing tight end now on offense, always fast for a kid his size, was right there with him, the two of them running shoulder to shoulder. Even Chris, who was supposed to lead the play, ran right past Palmer's outside linebacker, like he couldn't wait to get a piece of the cornerback, too.

Three Bulldogs buried *him* now.

Will could have walked home for the score. Will's dad sent Hannah in to kick the point, which she did. It was 36–14, the way it ended.

As they got into the line to shake hands with the Wildcats, Will said to Tim, "I thought you didn't want a girl on the team?"

"What's that mean?"

"It *means*," Will said, "that I was kind of surprised to see you turn into a heat-seeking missile on that block."

"Guy shouldn't have hit her like that, especially with the game over," Tim LeBlanc said. "That was messed up."

Tim took off his helmet.

"Might have played like a dog team for most of this game," he said. "We're still a team."

Maybe one that could learn something even when it lost.

18

There wasn't much talking inside Joe Tyler's car on the way home.

When they pulled into the parking lot, Hannah poked Will on the shoulder and said, "Talk to you?"

He thought he knew what might be coming. She had already told him after the game that she could have blocked the cornerback herself, that she could fight her own battles.

Will had said, "Actually, you can't always do that. Nobody can."

She was still in her pads and jersey. It still looked strange to Will, though, seeing her in uniform with her helmet off, long hair going down her back, reminding Will of a girl dressing up as a football player on Halloween.

Not that he was going to make that observation to her.

"I know you made Chris throw it to me," she said when it was just the two of them in front of the old gym, Wes and Ernie getting their helmets and pads out of the trunk of Joe Tyler's car.

"It's like I said to Chris," Will said. "I didn't think they'd expect it. And I wanted us to get that last score."

"Liar."

"Here we go again."

"You know it's true," she said. "But I don't even want to go there. But I do want you to make me a promise."

"What, that I won't ever change the play in the huddle ever again, whether I think you can get open or not?"

"No," she said. "I want you to promise me that I'm gonna be a real player on this team. Not just a kicker. Not somebody you needed to fill out the roster. It's like I told you: I want to *play*."

Will waited.

"I know I'm not great on defense, at least not yet. But I'm more than a kicker. You saw today that I *can* get open and catch the ball when it gets thrown to me. So I want you to promise that I'm not gonna be treated like some scrub. Because I'm not a scrub."

"Just because I called one play doesn't make me the new offensive coordinator," he said.

"Just promise," she said. Dug in. "I'd rather get hit like I got hit today than just stand out there sucking my thumb."

The fastest kid on the team and maybe the whole league knew he had nowhere to run.

"I promise," he said.

They shook on it, Hannah looking him right in the eyes as they did.

They saw Hannah's mom pull up next to Joe Tyler's car, saw her waving.

Hannah said, "I could have blocked that idiot myself, you know."

Then she gave Will a toss of that long hair, like she wanted to give him a good slap with it, and ran on long legs toward her mom's car.

Dinner with his dad wasn't a lot of laughs, either. There might have been slightly more conversation than the ride home. But not much.

Will had watched his dad on their sideline every chance he got today. Even though it was hard to think of it as a real sideline. Will wanted to see how his dad was taking it, losing the first game this way, being behind all day, having no realistic shot at winning in the second half. But if his dad, who hated to lose at anything, had dropped his guard, Will hadn't seen it. He kept encouraging them to the end, telling them not to quit, to keep running their stuff, to make a play whether they were on offense or defense.

Still.

The whole game Will kept thinking that he was the one who had talked his dad into doing this, who'd practically begged him to do this, and now they'd lost by three touchdowns and might have lost by more than that if Ryan Webb had kept throwing once his team had its big lead.

Near the end of dinner, pushing some of his Chinese takeout food around on his plate, Will's dad said, "It was good that the guys stuck up for her."

"It probably wasn't as much for Hannah as they just wanted to take out their frustration on somebody wearing a Palmer uniform," Will said.

"I was still glad."

"Dad, you wanted us to be better by the end of the game than we were at the start, and we were, right?"

"Right."

Will said, "Trust me, those guys on defense were trying on that last drive, I could tell they were, and we still took it to them."

"I was there, remember?" Joe Tyler smiled.

"And next Saturday will be better than this Saturday," Will said.

"All about the coaching," his dad said.

Will helped clean up, said he was going to turn in, he was beat, hugged Joe Tyler and told him he loved him and thanked him again for coaching the team.

Then he went upstairs and shut off the lights and stretched out on his bed, thinking that if it was all about the coaching, his dad better turn into a combination of Bill Belichick and Mike Tomlin of the Steelers between this Saturday and next Saturday.

Because next Saturday, the big bad Bears from Castle Rock were coming to town.

If the Bulldogs were underdogs against Palmer, what did that make them against Castle Rock?

19

They had a good week of practice, ending with them under the lights at Forbes High School on Friday night, Will's dad having gotten permission from the athletic director, another former teammate, the field being free because the high school team was on the road this week.

Will was still trying to recruit players every chance he got at school, not even wanting to think about actually going through a whole season without a single substitution, knowing how humiliated they were all going to feel the first time somebody got hurt and they were forced to play with ten players.

Or just forfeit the game.

The sign-up sheet stayed right where Will had posted it the first day outside the cafeteria at Forbes Middle. This week he had gone back to a couple of friends from the basketball team who weren't playing a fall sport this year, Dave Verkland and Brad Yarmouth, asking them if they'd changed their minds about playing football.

This was at lunch on Friday.

"Thrill," Dave said, "I'm not gonna risk my season for your season. I'm rooting for you, dude, but there's no way you guys finish the season."

"And don't you get hurt," Brad said, "because we're gonna need you at point guard."

"Nice talking to you," Will said, getting up from the table.

"Hey," Dave said, "we were just kidding around."

Only none of this was funny to Will.

On his way to math he saw Toby Keenan in the hall. Will had been giving Toby room, not pressuring him, hoping that he'd come around on his own. Now he asked him if he had a second, told him about getting shot down by Dave and Brad all over again, asked if Toby had given any more thought to not only joining the Bulldogs, but making them better the first day they got him into the uniform they were saving for him.

"I have thought about it," Toby said, staring down at his sneakers. "But I haven't changed my mind."

So the Bulldogs who showed up at Falcons Field on Friday night were the ones they'd play the season with, and that was that. *Fine*, Will thought. He told himself that he was going to stop worrying now about what they didn't have and be happy with what they did. Told himself that he was going to enjoy every practice and every game. Play for the love of the game now more than ever. He would stop worrying, at least for now, about another shot at Castle Rock in another West River championship game—and on what *planet* was that going to happen?—and just focus on the game he had tomorrow against them at Shea.

It had been hard for him losing to Palmer the way they had, Will knowing in his heart that the outcome would have been different if the sides had been remotely even, just in terms of numbers. But the sides weren't even. They weren't *going* to be even.

The only thing to do was play his hardest, get his teammates to play their hardest, try to have them all come together and be better than they thought they could be. Or were supposed to be. Because Will knew it happened that way in sports all the time, from the West River league all the way to the pros.

Maybe it was Friday night's practice being under the lights, making them feel older, like they were already on the high school team, that made it their very best practice so far. And Joe Tyler was the most fired up one on the field.

He could see the guys picking up on his 4-2-5 defense, and he'd added a couple of new trick plays on offense, even thrown in a fancy reverse on kickoff returns. Will's dad told the guys— and Hannah—that they were going to throw everything they had in their playbook at Castle Rock tomorrow.

"It's a pretty thin book, Mr. T.," Tim said.

Joe Tyler said, "Then we should be able to throw it even harder."

Practice was over by then. The players were kneeling around Will's dad, the way they did at the end of every practice.

"Listen," Joe Tyler said, "we've basically lost one core player from a team that should have beaten Castle Rock in last year's championship game, and that's Bobby Carrington. But what I saw against Palmer, that's maybe not going to be such a devastating loss, because I didn't see how we lost anything with Chris Aiello at QB."

It wasn't true. Will knew it and his dad knew it, because they'd talked about it. But he was trying to pump up his quarterback and now the Bulldogs did the same, clapping their hands.

"Those guys from Castle Rock are going to show up tomorrow thinking we have no shot," Joe Tyler said. "Anybody here think that?"

"No!"

"Well, then," he said, "I guess tonight's spot quiz is over and the only thing left to do is let the dogs out tomorrow afternoon."

Then they were all barking again, their coach included, probably making people who could hear them wonder what had gotten all the dogs in the neighborhood this worked up. Then they were all rolling in the grass, laughing at themselves and at each other.

Will didn't know what kind of team they were going to be this season, he really didn't.

But they were a team.

For now, that was enough.

It was 13–13 at halftime.

The Bulldogs had played them dead even almost from the time the Castle Rock Bears had gotten out of their green-and-white bus with the big bottle of Castle Rock water on the side.

Will had tried not to count the players getting off the bus, but thinking once they were all out, they might have brought enough guys to field three teams.

Defending champions of the West River league. Having brought Ben Clark, the best quarterback in the league, and Kendrick Morris, the best and loudest receiver. Having brought more fans across the river than the Bulldogs had, a *lot* more, and the Bulldogs were playing at home.

At least today the game was on a field that didn't make the home team ashamed. One of the things New Balance had done, at Joe Tyler's request, was invest in some rapid improvements to the conditions at Shea. New sod where it was needed. Newly chalked lines. Somehow, they'd even gotten the old scoreboard working again, a miracle that Will thought was the equivalent of sending a man to Mars.

Real field today. The Bulldogs playing like a real team. Against Castle Rock and against the odds, even if there was hardly anyone from Forbes to see it.

Ernie had sacked Ben Clark from his blind side early in the first quarter, forcing a fumble, Tim falling on the ball in the end zone. Hannah had stepped right up and kicked the extra point. Just like that it was 7–0.

The Bears responded with a long drive, though, Ben Clark finally hitting Kendrick Morris for the score. Will remembered Kendrick from last year's game because he'd made it impossible to forget him, the kid clearly thinking he was the West River version of Chad Ochocinco. If he made a first-down catch, he still jumped up and made the signal for the first down before the ref did.

And he was still talking the way he had last year, Kendrick being the one who did the most trash-talking when the game was over, making it a point to seek Will out and tell him that next year they were going to let him use a ball with a handle on it.

Ben Clark had told him after the championship game that Kendrick had gotten tired of the Castle Rock coaches telling him how fast Will was, how he was the guy they had to stop.

Ben had said, "He got it in his head that they were saying you were better than he was and, well, Kendrick doesn't think anybody is."

Will hated trash-talkers, always had, didn't respond last year and wasn't responding now. It didn't slow Kendrick Morris down even a little bit. Will was guarding him on the touchdown pass in the corner of the end zone, but Ben knew enough to throw it high, knowing Will wouldn't have a chance against a wide receiver who was bigger than he was and longer.

"Don't worry, little guy," Kendrick said. "It wasn't your fault. I'd give you a pat on the helmet, but I don't want to get flagged for fifteen on the kickoff."

Will wondered if a compliment might shut him up. Or at least slow him down. "Nice grab," he said.

"*Nice?*" Kendrick said. "Nice is for girls." Smiled at Will through his face mask and said, "But you know all about that, don't you, dog?"

Ben Clark kicked the point. 7–7. It stayed that way until half-way through the second quarter when Will took a handoff from Chris on a play called 34 Counter, did exactly what you're supposed to do, took a little jab step to his left that was the halfback version of a ball fake.

As soon as that got the defense leaning that way just enough, Will cut back to his right, picked up his blockers, saw even Hannah take out Castle Rock's safety with a solid block downfield. And then he was in the clear. He had scored last week against Palmer, but this was different, this was the first time he'd found that extra gear.

When he felt like he was flying down a football field again.

This was against Castle Rock. He turned after he handed the ball to the ref, pointed at Hannah because of her block. Kendrick Morris, who played both ways, played right corner on defense, must have thought Will had pointed at him, and from across the field, Will thought he might be yelling something.

He ignored it, listened to the cheers from the Forbes fans instead, got ready for the extra point. But Gerry Dennis, who held on placekicks, fumbled the snap, and the Bulldogs' lead was 13–7.

The Bears came right back again. In the last minute before halftime, on third-and-fourteen, Ben Clark threw one as far as he could to Kendrick, who had gotten behind Johnny Callahan, and by the time Kendrick showboated his way into the end zone, it was 13–all. Castle Rock went for two. Johnny read the play perfectly, stepped in front of Kendrick, knocked down Ben's pass.

Game tied.

On the Bulldogs' sideline, Joe Tyler got their attention and said, "There's not anybody I'm looking at who wouldn't have signed up for a tie game against those guys at the half. Now we just gotta figure out a way to keep rocking their world and beat them."

"You think that might stop Kendrick's chirping?" Tim said.

"I don't think he stops even when he's underwater," Chris said.

"We just gotta make sure we only have to say one word to him when the game's over," Will said. *"Scoreboard."*

"Well," Tim said, "now that it's working again."

"We're the ones who are gonna keep working," Will said, "all the way until we send them home in that bus of theirs *extremely* unhappy."

Will could see how tired his teammates were getting the longer the game went on. But the game was still even, at 20–20, in the fourth quarter. Castle Rock got their score on an all-out blitz on one of Hannah's punts, blocking it, recovering in the end zone, Ben kicking the point.

But this time it was the Bulldogs who responded with a long drive, one even better than the last drive the week before against Palmer. Will's dad would tell them it was twelve plays and seventy-six yards when it was over, six runs and six passes, even one to Hannah for a first down on third-and-four from midfield.

They finally scored from the eight-yard line. Will ended up

with the ball on 38 Toss, Quarterback Throw, running to his right. But Ben Clark knew the play and got back to cover Chris as he circled out of the backfield on the left and then turned up the field.

So Will pulled the ball down, broke a tackle, dove for the right pylon, actually put the ball right on top of it.

Hannah's kick was center cut.

Eight minutes left, Bulldogs 20, Bears 20, at Shea.

Even Will Tyler, the biggest believer of all, couldn't believe it. When Ben had come over to shake his hand before the game, he couldn't resist saying, "Hey, who picked these teams?"

More than anything, Will just wanted to repeat that line to Ben when the game was over. Telling himself that it wasn't trash talk if you were just *repeating* something, was it?

They just needed a couple of stops. Needed to have the ball in their hands at the end. Make it one of those games, the best kind of football game, last team with the ball wins.

As long as it was your team.

This time, Will told himself, *I'm not fumbling the game away.* He had no idea if he'd ever get near a rematch in the championship game with these guys. So maybe this was as good as it was going to get against Castle Rock this season, trying to win the championship of *today.* Not best-of-seven or anything like that. Best of the forty minutes they played in the West River league.

The Bulldogs needed a stop. But Will could see how tired the other guys were, especially the guys up front, the ones who'd been taking a pounding all day from offensive and defensive linemen from Castle Rock, guys who looked as if they were in high school already.

The Castle Rock coaches saw it the same as Will did. The same as everybody at Shea had to see it. So as good a thrower as Ben was, the Bears started to grind it out, running the ball on almost every down and daring the Bulldogs to stop them. Five yards here, six yards there, eating up yardage, eating up the clock.

The one time they ended up with a third-and-eight, though, everybody knew it was a passing situation. Will lined up on Kendrick. Ben threw it high again. Kendrick went up for it and came down with the first down.

Made his first-down gesture, like always.

"Now say somethin'," Kendrick said.

"I wasn't talking to you before," Will said.

"I'd call that a tall tale," Kendrick said, "but you're too little."

Two minutes to play. Castle Rock ball on the Forbes thirty-yard line.

Before he got to his huddle, Kendrick turned and said, "Tell your boys—and the girl—that you've had all the fun you're gonna have today."

Ben came right back to Kendrick again, surprising Will with a first-down pass. Will was lucky to knock him out-of-bounds on the ten. Ben scored two plays later on a quarterback draw but hooked the extra point kick badly to the left.

26–20, Castle Rock. Sixty-five seconds left in the game.

If the Bulldogs could score, if Hannah could kick the point . . .

But there was a lot of work to do before that.

Less work after Will broke up the middle on the kickoff, cut to the right sideline, returned the ball all the way to the Bears' forty-five-yard line.

Under a minute now.

Hannah spoke in a huddle for the first time, right before Chris called their first-down play.

"Let's rock the Rock," she said.

On first down, Castle Rock expecting a pass, Joe Tyler had Chris pitch it to Will, who got to the edge for ten yards. Chris had called two plays in the huddle, so they lined up quickly and Will went off tackle for ten more, cutting to the outside. He tried to get out-of-bounds this time to stop the clock but couldn't, so the Bulldogs were forced to burn their last time-out.

Thirty-five seconds left.

They were on the twenty-five now. Even the way Will was eating up yards, he knew they couldn't keep running the ball, not without time-outs. Chris, who'd never played quarterback before this season, who'd never been in this position before, was going to have to take some shots at the end zone soon.

On first down, Chris scrambled out of the pocket to his right, then back to his left, finally overthrew Johnny on the left sideline. On second down, though, Chris floated a ball perfectly over one of their linebackers, hit Tim right in stride.

But at the last second Tim took his eyes off the ball, wanting to see what was up ahead of him. The ball went right through his hands.

Third-and-ten. Ball still on the Bears twenty-five. Fifteen seconds on the clock. Chris pump-faked beautifully as if he really was going to take a shot at the end zone, then turned and dumped the ball to Will in the flat. Will caught it, spun away from their outside linebacker. There was daylight in the middle of the field, but he couldn't risk going there; if he didn't make the end zone, he was afraid the game would be over before Chris could get them lined up and spike the ball.

Will managed to get out-of-bounds at the seven.

Five seconds left.

Chris looked over to Will's dad for the play. One play to tie, to give Hannah a chance to win it with an extra point. "Draw play," Chris said.

"Love it," Will said.

Will shot a quick look at his dad. It was as if Joe Tyler was waiting for his son to look over. He nodded. Behind him, Will could see everybody in the stands, whether they were rooting for Forbes or Castle Rock, on their feet.

Will thought: *This is why I wrote the letter.*

This is why you play.

Chris pulled away from center as if he was going to drop back to pass again. But then he spun and put the ball on Will's belly.

The middle linebacker ran right past Will, going for the quarterback all the way. The hole was there now. The end zone right in front of Will.

He never saw Kendrick Morris coming from the side.

Just felt his legs go out from underneath him as Kendrick came into him with the rolling block that was as sure as a tackle.

Will kept his feet as long as he could, made sure to hold on to the ball, still felt as if he could make it even as he felt himself falling.

He came down at the one-yard line.

Hit the ground and heard the ref's whistle as soon as he did, telling everybody at Shea that the game was over, that the Bulldogs had come up one touchdown short of Castle Rock.

One yard short.

20

The ball was still sitting there in front of Will, at least until Kendrick Morris booted it away.

Somehow Will wasn't even surprised. The guy didn't even know how to act after making a simple first down; why would anything be different now? Helping his team win a great game like this didn't make him any less of a loser.

"Choked it down again, didn't you?" Kendrick said.

"Thanks for sharing, Kendrick," Will said.

"All I ever hear about is how fast you are, how to beat Forbes we got to beat the great Will Tyler, how lucky we were to beat you last year," Kendrick said, loud enough to be heard all over the field.

Ben Clark walked up now, tried to pull Kendrick away, telling him to chill.

"I don't have to chill," Kendrick said. "We won."

Ben Clark said, "We don't want to win like this."

"You didn't have to tell me how to win the game," Kendrick said to his own teammate. "Don't tell me what to do now."

Kendrick looked at Will and said, "Who was the one could fly with the game on the line?" He banged his chest hard and said, "Special K was."

Now one of the refs came walking over. "Son," he said to Kendrick, "if I give you an unsportsmanlike conduct penalty after the game is over, you miss your next game. So I want you to zip it and walk away."

Kendrick walked away but had one more thing to say, just loud enough for Will to hear.

"Who's the one can really fly?" Kendrick said.

Then he was off and running, making the flying motion that Braylon Edwards of the Jets made when his team won a big game.

"Don't listen to that jerk," Tim said when Will was sitting with his teammates in front of their bench.

"Hard not to," Will said. "I think they could hear him on the other side of the river."

Joe Tyler came over then, pulled his son to his feet, pressed his forehead against Will's helmet. "You were great today," his dad said.

"We still lost."

"People will still remember how you played. That's what they remember. What you do, not what you say."

The coach of the Bulldogs told them to all gather around him then, told them how proud he was of them, told them they became a real team today.

Then the Bulldogs, as much as the loss had hurt, were ripping into the snacks that Johnny Callahan's mother had brought, chips and cookies and even homemade brownies. But Will didn't want anything to eat or drink. He wanted to go home, go up to his room, close the door, deal with coming up one yard short against Castle Rock.

A loss like this?

Will didn't let go right away.

He took off his helmet, quietly slipped away from his teammates, walked around the bleachers, on his way to wait for his dad in the car.

But one last time today, there was Kendrick Morris. Like he thought he had to cover Will all the way to the parking lot.

"Know what the best part was?" Kendrick said, starting right in.

He had taken his shoulder pads and jersey off, was just wearing a gray T-shirt with his football pants. He'd taken off his cleats, but even in socks, he was bigger than Will. Smiling at him. One of the meanest smiles Will had ever seen.

Mean kid.

"What?" Will said in a tired voice.

"That you thought you had the game right before I snatched it back," Kendrick said, pulling his arm back. "*That* was the best part."

"Glad that rang your bell," Will said.

"Oh yeah."

And in that moment, Will couldn't help himself any longer.

"Can I ask *you* a question?" he said.

"Now you know I got answers for anything you throw my way, right? But go ahead, it pleases you."

Will was the one smiling now. "Do you think we should stop talking before somebody starts to think *I'm* the jerk?"

It seemed to take a moment for it to register with Kendrick that he'd been insulted, maybe because of the pleasant tone of voice Will had used.

But when it did, Kendrick's smile disappeared and he was coming for Will, saying as he did, "You want some of me, little man?"

He came up a yard short.

Because Toby Keenan stepped out from the bleachers as if appearing out of nowhere, stepped right between Kendrick and Will.

"Beat it," he said to Kendrick Morris.

Maybe it was the way Toby said it. Or the look on his face. Maybe it was just the size of him, towering over Kendrick the way he did.

The best Kendrick could do was, "Who are you?"

"The guy telling you to beat it. Unless you want a piece of me the way you wanted a piece of him."

Kendrick opened his mouth, closed it, turned just like that and walked around the corner of the bleachers, moving so.

quickly it was like he was suddenly afraid he might miss the team bus.

Gone.

"He shouldn't have yelled at you," Toby said. "I hate guys who yell like that."

"Me too."

It was still just the two of them behind the bleachers. Maybe the quiet between them seemed more pronounced because Kendrick was gone.

"What are you doing here?" Will said finally.

"I want to play," Toby said.

21

I t turned out that Joe Tyler had done a good job guessing the sizes Toby would need for equipment if he ever did decide to play, including his head size for the helmet. The only place he guessed wrong was with the shoes. The ones he ordered were too small.

Even with that the shoes weren't big enough.

Joe Tyler told him, no worries, he'd contact New Balance in the morning and Toby would probably have his new shoes in time for Wednesday's practice.

"I'll tell them I need them ASAP for my game changer," Will's dad said.

Toby looked down, the way he did a lot, Will had noticed. "I don't know about that, Mr. Tyler."

"I tell Will all the time I can teach a lot of things on a football field," Will's dad said. "But no coach in history, not one of the guys who coached the Steelers to the Super Bowl, has ever been able to teach big and fast."

"You know how announcers are always talking about fans in a loud stadium being a team's twelfth man?" Will said. "You're gonna be a *way* different kind of twelfth man for us now."

They were in the living room, shoe boxes open on the floor, Toby wearing his brand-new football pants, helmet and shoulder pads in front of him on the coffee table. When he'd been standing next to Joe Tyler, Will noticed that he was just as tall. And looked a whole lot broader.

Toby made their living room feel even smaller than normal just by being in it.

Will's dad said, "Can I ask you what changed your mind, if you don't mind telling me? I mean, other than that Kendrick kid running his mouth at Will the way he did?"

Now Toby looked up.

"I watched the game," he said.

"I didn't see you," Will said.

"Didn't want you to. I just wanted to see the team play for myself."

Neither Will nor his dad said anything now, letting Toby tell it his own way. Will was wondering how much of an effort it took just for Toby to show up at the field, much less make the decision to get back in the game.

"I saw how hard you guys fought," Toby said to Will. "When the game started, I thought you had no chance. Castle Rock, they just had more of . . . *everything*. But somehow you stayed with them. Then as the game went along, I can't explain it, but I started to see myself out there. Especially on their last drive, when one stop could have made the difference. And I'd always been taught—by my mom, anyway, before she left—that if you think you can make a difference in something, you have to try."

Toby shrugged, tried to smile. "All I got," he said.

"I'm glad," Will said.

"We're all glad," his dad said.

Then Toby said, "Mr. Tyler, you know about my dad."

"I know your dad, son. My whole life."

"So you know what he's like."

"Yeah, I know what he's like when he gets around football."

Will looked at the big guy, biggest in their grade by far, like he'd grown nine more sizes since he'd last played football in the fifth grade, somehow looking like a scared little kid talking about his own father.

Will thought: *And I think I've got problems in my life.*

Toby said in a small voice, "I'm not gonna be able to keep him from coming to games."

"Did you tell him you were going to play?"

"Last night, when I got home."

"Was he happy to hear it?" Will's dad said.

Toby made a snorting sound. "Not too much makes my dad happy."

"What did he say?" Will said.

"That it was about time I decided to man up; they already had one girl on the team."

"You know how they call some guys 'monster backs' in football?" Tim said to Will. "Dude, Toby really puts the monster in it."

"Troy Polamalu, just without the hair," Will said.

This was Monday night at practice, Toby's first with the Bulldogs. Jeremiah, who'd spent most of the practice trying in vain to block Toby Keenan in what were now six-on-six drills, said, "I think the big guy and Polamalu are already the same size."

Everybody on the field could see how Toby looked even bigger in football gear. But he was faster than Will remembered. And quick. Will knew there was a difference in sports; you could be one without being the other. There were guys on the Bulldogs who were fast over thirty or forty yards but not quick enough to the ball on defense, not quick enough with the kind of short burst you needed to fill a hole you saw opening a few yards in front of you.

Toby was both.

Big-time.

Maybe the most amazing thing, an hour into practice, was this: not only did he not look as if he'd taken a season off from football, he looked as if he hadn't missed a single practice. On top of that, it had only taken him one night of studying to learn all the plays Will's dad had sent him home with on Sunday.

It was as if he'd been waiting all this time to let all the football he had inside him *out*. To run around like this and hit people again and be a player again. And just maybe, Will thought, to be a part of something. Toby still wasn't saying much—other than "Sorry" sometimes when he'd level somebody new and immediately help him up—and never joked around between plays the way Tim and some of the other guys did.

And still, just watching him, Will felt like this was as happy as Toby ever got.

"You know what the challenge is gonna be?" Joe Tyler said to Will during a water break, with Toby out of earshot.

"Waiting until Saturday to see him in a real game?" Will said.

"Figuring out where he can help us the most on offense," Joe Tyler said.

Will knew what his dad meant. Defense was a no-brainer; he was going to be in the middle of their 4-2-5, a monster back in all ways, moving around the field and terrorizing offenses the way Polamalu did or the way Clay Matthews of the Packers, another guy with insanely long hair, did.

But on offense? Will could see him at left tackle, protecting Chris's blind side. Or fullback. Even though he looked like more of a tight end than a wideout, Will couldn't help dreaming about a rematch with Castle Rock. Imagine what it would be like watching Kendrick Morris try to match up with Toby in a game instead of in back of the bleachers.

"For now I'm thinking tight end," Joe Tyler said. "See if there are any linebackers in the West River league who can run with him or any safeties who want to hit him."

In their first two games Will's dad had been moving his receivers around. Hannah was always at one wide receiver position, but he'd been swapping off Johnny and Tim at the other one, even throwing Gerry Dennis out there sometimes. It was Joe Tyler's way of mixing things up, giving the other team different looks. But for the last half hour of practice tonight, the Bulldogs first walking through their plays and then running through them with the orange cones, he had them line up this way:

Toby at tight end. Johnny at one wide receiver, Tim at the other, Hannah sitting out.

Joe Tyler had made sure to tell Hannah exactly what he was doing, trying to make it sound like a good thing that she wasn't out there right now.

"I know you have the plays down cold," Will's dad said, "probably even better than my own kid. So you take a break and let Toby see what it looks like to have them up and running on the field. Okay?"

"No problem," Hannah said.

Will wasn't so sure. Before they ran their first play, he watched her move to the side, take off her helmet, give her hair a shake, put the helmet on her hip. No expression on her face. But when the play was over, a simple buttonhook to Toby, and Will looked over at her again, he saw her staring straight at him.

Like he'd done something.

When practice was over, Hannah waited until she could get Will alone. On the field, Chris and Toby were doing some extra

CHAPTER

22

F rom the start of Saturday's game against Cannondale, you could see that Toby Keenan was back in football in a big way.

For the Bulldogs that wasn't just good news, it was great news, on both sides of the ball.

That's what you could see. What you could hear was that his dad was back, too.

Bad news.

Dick Keenan didn't start in right away; the first time Will really became aware of him was early in the second quarter, when Chris tried to throw Toby an underneath pass on Go-7-Go, both Hannah and Johnny having taken off down the field ahead of him on fly patterns.

By then, it was 14–0 for the Bulldogs, Will having scored one touchdown on a thirty-two-yard run the first time they had the ball. Toby had scored the other on what Will thought was a pretty amazing catch, going up between a safety and a linebacker and coming down with the ball in the back of the end zone, managing to keep two feet inbounds.

"What's the next step up from monster?" Tim said.

"Him," Will said.

But now on what looked like a much simpler catch, Toby got hit from the side just as the ball arrived, the Cannondale middle linebacker timing his hit perfectly and knocking the ball loose.

First ball he hadn't caught in his first game back. Toby was still playing like he'd practiced, like he'd never been away.

"Concentrate!"

Toby's dad.

"You think they're gonna just go home because you made a couple of plays on them?"

Will looked over to the bleachers, Toby's dad back at his old perch, last row. Nobody close to him.

"You go over the middle, you gotta expect to be hit. Protect the stinkin' ball!"

Will knew Toby was hearing this, the way everybody else at Shea was. Will's dad had always said that you couldn't have what he called "rabbit ears" in sports, that you couldn't waste your time listening to what the other players were saying or the people in the stands.

But how could you not have rabbit ears when it was your *own* dad?

Toby, to his credit, didn't let it show, didn't let on that his dad was yelling at him this way. He'd known it was coming if *he* came back and now here it was, first time he screwed up.

Three plays later, Chris threw him the same pass. Toby got hit again. This time he held on to the ball. Not only did he hold on, he turned upfield, proceeded to run over three Cannondale tacklers on his way to a sixty-five-yard scoring play, knocking them over like they were orange cones at practice.

"Well," Will said to Tim after Hannah kicked the point, "now we know what happens when you make the big guy mad."

Tim was running alongside Will to where Hannah would kick off. "But what must it be like to go through life with *that* in your ear?"

"And in your face," Will said.

By halftime it was 28–7. Over the rest of the second quarter, Toby's dad was still the loudest voice in the stands, by far. He didn't always criticize, but when Toby would get another sack or make another open-field tackle or make another catch, the best he could hope to hear was this:

"That's more like it."

Or:

"That's the way I taught you."

Like somehow he was the one out on the field. Will found himself wondering if that was the problem, that he wasn't out there anymore. And wondering something else: if on Dick Keenan's best day he was even half the player that his son was.

The Cannondale quarterback looked around before every

snap, making sure he knew where Toby was. Joe Tyler tried to make it hard for the poor kid, moving Toby around, putting him in a three-point stance on the line sometimes, dropping him back into coverage, blitzing him every chance he got.

At halftime Will said to Toby, "Dude, you were awesome out there."

Toby said, "It'll be better in the second half."

"I don't know how you could play much better."

"No," Toby said, "my dad's gone. He has to do some tree work today."

"You just keep doing what you're doing," Will said.

Toby pushed back his helmet, gave Will a long look. He started to say something, stopped, finally said, "I'll try."

Will knew he had to have way more than a hundred rushing yards at half. Just having another threat like Toby on the field made things so much easier for him, didn't allow Cannondale to load up the box the way most teams did against the Bulldogs. When they did, Chris would fake the ball to Will and throw it to Toby.

Toby wasn't doing it alone on defense, either. Just by showing up, getting in there at linebacker next to Matt, backing up Jeremiah and Ernie and Wes and Jake in the D line, he was doing what big players—and not just big in size—were supposed to do in sports:

Make everybody around them better.

And he was helping in another way: giving the other Bulldogs a chance to take a few plays off. Joe Tyler picked his spots resting people, but even getting short breathers seemed to help by the time they got to the second half.

When Will scored his third touchdown of the day; it was 35–13. After that, Chris started handing the ball to Gerry Dennis when the Bulldogs were on offense. In the fourth quarter, Will's dad switched Will out to wide receiver and put Tim in the backfield, letting him have five or six carries on their last drive.

After Tim broke off a ten-yard run, he came back into the huddle and said to Will, "Look at me, I've turned into *you!*"

"I don't recall ever playing and doing play-by-play at the same time," Will said.

"So sad," Tim said, "a hater even as we're getting our first win."

It stayed at 35–13. On this day, the Bulldogs could have scored more, run *up* the score if they'd wanted to. But Will's dad wasn't that kind of coach. He knew they were never going to be that kind of team.

As Will watched the last seconds tick off the clock, took one last look at the final score, he felt himself smiling. This time he felt himself flying even though he was standing still.

They were on the board.

23

L ittle by little, Will saw his dad loving football again.

He wasn't sure if his dad would ever come out and say that, or if he was even thinking about it that way. But Will knew what he was seeing.

Joe Tyler still came home tired—and limping—after work. Still had to stretch out on the couch or on his bed if it had been a day when he'd been delivering the mail on foot instead of from the truck. Will had asked his dad one time why he wasn't always in the truck and his dad said that the rest of the guys alternated between walking and riding, and he wasn't going to ask for any special favors.

But when it was time to go to practice, it was like he'd turned into a different guy. A new man almost. Limping sometimes, but never looking tired.

Joe Tyler even knew how to get on guys, with humor, never with shouting. He'd promised Will he wasn't going to be that

kind of coach and had kept his promise. It seemed more important than ever now that Toby Keenan was on the team.

And his dad knew how to praise guys, at practice and at games,
without ever overdoing it, so that the words meant something.

In a way, Will thought, it was the same with his dad as it was
with Toby:

All the football he'd carried inside him was coming out again.

And maybe his best coaching was with Hannah, which was
why what was supposed to be one of the big issues of the
season—having a girl on the team—seemed to be getting
smaller all the time.

Will knew she didn't get as many passes thrown her way as
she would have liked, but even she knew that Johnny was a better receiver than she was, and that's why more balls went his
way. When a well-thrown ball did come her way, she held on to
it. And showed she could take a good hit. And the other players
on the team noticed that she never ran out-of-bounds to avoid a
hit if she thought she could make more yardage.

She got in on tackles, too, even made some of her own in the
open field.

"I was wrong about her," Tim said to Will when they were
warming up before the Merrell game. "Even though I will be
forced to deny that if you ever try to tell anybody."

"Your secret is safe with me," Will said. "You big phony."

Tim ignored the last part. "Not only can she play like a guy,"
he said, "she's as tough as most guys we know."

Will said, "She doesn't look at it that way. She thinks we're just trying to be as tough as her."

The Merrell game turned out to be the roughest of the season by far. And occasionally—on the part of the Merrell players—the dirtiest.

There were a lot of penalties called in the first half. Just *stuff*, usually at the bottom of the pile when the refs couldn't see what was going on. One time Merrell's middle linebacker stepped on Will's hand after Will had gained a hard three yards on third down, clearly doing it on purpose even though he said, "My bad," when he made a fake show of helping Will up. There was another time, again at the bottom of the pile, when the last guy up for the Merrell Lions "accidentally" pushed Will's face into the turf as he got to his feet.

Will never said anything or tried to retaliate, just kept picking himself up, going back to the huddle, asking for the ball again, knowing the best way to answer them was with his legs and not his mouth.

But he could see the Merrell Lions getting more and more frustrated when they couldn't score against the defenses Joe Tyler kept throwing at them. It was why he didn't think the second half was going to get any easier against these guys, was pretty sure the chippy stuff was only going to get worse, especially after Hannah caught her first touchdown pass of the season right before the end of the half.

She'd beaten the cornerback covering her with a neat move

and broke to the corner of the end zone, Chris delivering the ball perfectly. Hannah had just enough room to get both feet down inbounds, making sure to land on her toes, just like the pros did.

The play should have been over, but it wasn't. The cornerback clearly didn't like being beaten that way by a girl. Hannah had slowed down after running out of the end zone but still hadn't turned around when the cornerback went piling into her, sending her sliding into the chain-link fence that was close to the field at that end.

Tim started to run at the cornerback, but Will grabbed him from behind before he did, pulling him toward where Hannah was already getting up and waving them off like it was no big deal.

"You okay?" Will said.

"Believe me," she said, "I've run into bigger jerks than that guy."

But Will noticed her limping slightly on her left leg when she set up for the extra point, wincing as she tried to plant her foot, barely getting the ball through the uprights.

Bulldogs 7–0 at the half.

Right before Will went out to receive the second-half kick, his dad pulled him aside.

"Listen," he said to Will, "I'll take the hit on this, but I'm not gonna play her very much the rest of the way. This has turned into the kind of game my old coach used to call a triple-chin-strap game and I'm afraid the next time she gets clobbered like that, she's not gonna get up."

"She won't be happy," Will said. "Trust me."

"Trust *me*, her parents won't be happy if their daughter comes home in a sling."

"I hear you."

The game stayed 7–0 until midway through the fourth quarter when Will took a pitch from Chris on 38 Toss, found a gaping hole and took the thing to the house, sixty-eight yards. On the extra-point attempt, one of the Lions' outside linebackers got around Jeremiah, blocked the kick and kept running right through Hannah.

She took even longer to get up this time than she had when she went into the fence after her touchdown.

When she came off, Will's dad said to her, "Now you're totally done for the day."

"I'm fine," she said.

He said, "There are times when you wait to fight another day, and this is gonna have to be one of them."

The Bulldogs eventually ran out the last five minutes of the game with a drive that took them from their thirty to the Lions' thirty. Every once in a while, Will looked over and saw Hannah next to his dad, obviously trying to get back into the game.

Sometimes he would smile and shake his head.

Finally he just walked away.

It *had* been hard fought, but the Bulldogs had evened their record at 2–2.

The trip to Merrell was their longest of the season, nearly an hour. They didn't get back to Forbes Middle until five o'clock.

At six, the doorbell rang and when Will opened their front door, Hannah was standing there.

"We need to talk," she said.

Will's dad had gone to the gym as soon as they got home, saying he was going to torture himself, that he'd been slacking off lately.

"It finally happened," she said. "I got treated differently today."

"You got hurt today."

"So did Ernie," she said. "Did he sit out the second half?"

The Lions' fullback had gotten called for a tripping penalty halfway through the third quarter when Ernie had a clear path to the quarterback. He rolled his ankle going down and let out a howl of pain, but when Will asked him if he needed to come out, Ernie grinned.

"If I do, who buries that sucker on the next play?" he said, and played on.

Will grinned. "The only pain Ernie feels is when he can't come up with an answer in class."

"Your dad didn't even think about replacing him," she said. "But he treats me like a delicate flower."

"We can't afford to lose you," Will said.

"Right."

"I mean it. You got crushed after the touchdown. And then you got crushed again on the blocked punt. And I know you got hurt both times even though you won't admit it."

"It's tackle football, remember? Everybody gets hurt."

"Why can't you be happy that you scored a touchdown?"

"How come he didn't protect *you*?" Hannah said. "You took more hard hits today than you did all season. And you're not as big as I am."

"Seriously?" Will said. "We're gonna play that game?"

"No," she said. "We're just replaying today's game." They were in the living room, at both ends of the couch. It felt to Will like they were fighters looking at each other from different corners.

She shook her head. "A couple of jerks give me a couple of cheap shots and now I get treated differently."

Will took a deep breath. "You're the one acting like a jerk."

"Excuse me?"

"I listened to you, now you listen to me," he said. "Did you join this team to prove a point or to win the game?"

"Win the game," she said. "But that's *not* the point."

"Yeah," he said, "it is. We won the game today. You played great. Why did my dad sit you down? Because he doesn't just coach one game, he coaches the whole season, and if you get seriously hurt, then we lose our kicker and one of our best receivers and a pretty good defensive back and we're back to eleven guys."

She said, "Your dad thought we could get by with eleven guys in the second half today, didn't he?"

"Man, you're tough."

"You knew that already."

"You're right, totally," Will said. "You're the toughest girl I've ever seen in sports, not that I've watched a lot of girl sports. And you're the best by far."

"Woo hoo," she said.

Will said, "Do you always go out of your way to make it this hard for somebody to like you?"

As soon as he said it, he wished he'd found another way. Anything but *like*. You could use that word anytime you wanted with a bud. With a guy. You could say how much you liked a video game or a song you'd just downloaded or a funny website or say how much you liked your favorite team.

You never used *like* with a girl.

Especially not this girl, who let nothing slide.

"You *like* me?" she said.

Will took a deep breath, let it out, smiled at her, ran his hands through his hair, pushed his chair back a little, the legs making a loud scraping sound. "Well, yeah, obviously," he said. "I mean, I'm trying."

"You like me for real, or you just worried I might up and quit on you one of these days?"

"I know you well enough to know you'd never quit," he said. "You like playing too much. And I *really* like that."

She had her hair back in a ponytail. Was wearing cutoff jeans. And a T-shirt that read: "I'm Unique (Just Like Everyone Else)."

"And besides," Will said, "you need this team as much as it needs you."

"Wait a second," Hannah said. "*I* need *you*?"

"Yeah," Will said, "you do. Unless you think that in four games you already proved you're as good as you think you are."

Hannah smiled then. The kind of smile that first got Will to even *think* about liking her in a way he'd never thought about liking a girl before.

"Not a bad point."

"One in a row," he said.

"Your dad *did* treat me like a girl today; don't try to deny it."

Will couldn't help it now; he laughed. As soon as he did, he put his hands up, as if in self-defense, and said, *"You are a girl!"*

"Who wants to be treated like everybody else," she said, stubborn to the end.

"I get that," Will said. "But more than that, you want to win as much as I do. As much as anybody on the team does. And my dad says that sometimes you've got to make sacrifices to win, whether you want to or not, for the *good* of the team."

She said, "You really buy into all that team stuff, don't you?"

"I do," Will said. "But you do, too. I see how hard you compete. I see you try to make tackles even knowing you're going to get run over. It's why I know it's more than you just proving your point about being as good as boys in sports. You want to do this as much as I do."

"You're saying I'm like you?"

Will nodded.

"Well," she said, "like you only *taller.*"

"Here we go again."

She smiled. "Sometimes I can't help myself."

Will said, "We can beat Castle Rock. I wouldn't have said it at the start of the year. But I'm saying it now. We can get back to the championship game and beat them."

"You're going to need me," she said.

"My point," he said.

They were silent after that.

Then Hannah stood up suddenly. "I have to go," she said.

"We good?"

She nodded. "Just tell your dad to leave me in there next time," she said. "I can take care of myself."

"Deal."

Will stood up. They shook hands for the second time this season. Then he walked her to the front door.

"See you at school," he said.

"And then practice," Hannah said.

"Cool."

He opened the front door for her.

When she was halfway down the walk, she turned and said, "I like you, too."

Then she cut across the lawn like she was evading a tackler and sprinted up Valley Road, Will still smiling even after she had disappeared.

24

When dinner was over, Will told his dad he was going to take a walk to Shea.

"Don't you ever get tired?" his dad said.

"Yeah," Will said. "But I'm like you. I don't let anybody see."

"I *wish*," his dad said, and told him to head out, he'd clean up by himself; when Will came back, they could watch the Saturday night college football game. Will asked who was playing and Joe Tyler said, "Who cares? It's a game, we're guys, it's on TV, it's practically our duty to watch."

Will wasn't sure why he needed to be outside, move around, get some air. But he did. He took his ball with him, more by force of habit than anything else. He noticed on the way to Shea how quiet the streets were, even early on a Saturday night. He didn't even see many cars on the road. It was one of those quiet moments in Forbes when you wondered if everybody had left.

One more of his dreams for the end of the season? That there would be this huge crowd if they made it to the championship game, that the whole town would come out and cheer them on if they got their rematch against Castle Rock. Last year the championship game had been on their field. But it was a league rule, Will knew, that you couldn't host the big game two years in a row, even if you had the best record the way Castle Rock did now, still undefeated.

What would that be like, Will wondered now at Shea, looking at the empty bleachers and the empty field, having the whole town get behind them? What would it be like if they could give Forbes something to cheer about again?

But tonight Shea was silent, nobody around. Will was half-hoping that Hannah would show up, had even thought about calling her, asking if she wanted to meet up with him. But he wimped out. It had been a good day with her already. No. A *great* day. And he decided to just leave it alone.

I like you, too, she'd said.

To Will it felt almost as big as the win over Merrell.

Big day all around. One of the best he'd had in a long time.

He put the ball under his arm and jogged straight up the middle of the field, no cuts or stops, then turned and came back the other way. It didn't look like some field that football had forgotten anymore. It still wasn't Heinz Field. It wasn't Castle Rock's turf field. Will knew there were still potholes waiting to trip him up when he least expected it. But with the new sod and the fresh chalk and even the new goalposts that New Balance had surprised them with, it looked like a real field again.

Real field, real team.

Their next game was here next Saturday. And if the Bulldogs could beat the Becker Falls Panthers, they were tied with them for second place in the league. And if they could win out the rest of the way, they were back in the championship game; the play-offs in the West River league were just one game:

No. 1 in the standings versus No. 2.

Will stood there in the end zone, smiling, thinking about how far they'd all come in a month.

They hadn't won anything yet. Even now, this far into the season, just four regular-season games left, Will was still trying to find reinforcements. Still worried about one of his teammates—Toby in particular—getting hurt.

Or two guys getting hurt.

Joe Tyler had checked with the league, just making sure: they could play with ten if they ever had to. But with every game the rest of the way feeling like a playoff game, that would be a total disaster.

What if somebody went down next week against Becker Falls? Or against Castle Rock, if they made it that far?

Stop it.

Will thought of one of his dad's favorite expressions: You want to make God laugh? Tell Him about your plans. His dad knew better than anybody, because the plans he'd had for his life hadn't turned out anything like he'd expected them to, or wanted them to.

For now, Will stretched out in the end zone, put his ball underneath his head like a pillow. It wasn't dark yet, but Will could still see the first stars in the sky.

For tonight he wasn't going to worry about what might go wrong; he was going to think about what was going right, what a great season it had been so far. Oh, he wished they could have beaten Castle Rock, no doubt, wished he hadn't come up a yard short against those guys. But he knew he would have signed up for a record of 2–2 when the season started, signed up for the chance to go into second place next Saturday, knowing that a win would give the Bulldogs the tiebreaker on Becker Falls as long as they kept winning.

Today they'd even gotten lucky with Toby's obnoxious dad; he'd decided not to make the trip to Merrell.

Yeah, life was good.

And had he mentioned in the past few minutes that Hannah Grayson said she liked him?

"Hey."

The voice startled him. But he recognized it right away.

Tim.

"Hey, Thrill."

As soon as Will sat up, Will could see from Tim LeBlanc's face that something was wrong. Real wrong. Will thinking he looked the way he had the first time they'd watched *The Express* together, because Tim hadn't known that Ernie Davis was going to die in the end, either.

"Don't worry," Tim had said that day. "You're never gonna see me cry."

Until now.

"We're moving," Tim said.

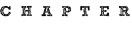

T his wasn't about losing a player.

This was about losing the player who was his best friend, from the first day of first grade and every day since then.

Losing him to Scottsdale, Arizona. In eight days. All because his dad had gotten a better job, a much better job, at a software company there.

Tim explained it all to Will, how if his dad hadn't said yes right away, somebody else's family would be moving to Scottsdale. How the company had already found them a house to rent while they looked at one to buy. How it was already arranged that Tim and his sister could start at the best middle school in Scottsdale a week from Monday.

"You think you're fast, Thrill?" Tim said. "This all happened faster."

Will knew Tim's dad was always sending out job applications, tired of having to commute to Pittsburgh, tired of living half his life in his car. And, according to Tim, never believing the job in Pittsburgh would last; that's why Mr. LeBlanc hadn't moved them there.

But now they were moving to Arizona. Done deal. Tim's dad had found out that morning, but wanted to wait until after the Merrell game to tell Tim and his sister. Tim said he'd called Will right away, but he'd already left for Shea.

Now here they were, just the two of them, the way it had been so many other times in their lives. Just never like this.

"We leave next Sunday," Tim said. "My dad said I can still play in the Becker Falls game, on account of it being such a big game."

"I don't care about the stupid game!" Will said, the force of his own words surprising him. "I care about you leaving!"

"The first thing I told my dad when he told us was that I couldn't leave the team," Tim said. "And he said he understood how I felt, but we were a family, and from the first day, we were gonna start our new life together as a family."

"I liked your old life just fine," Will said.

"Same," Tim said. "Trust me."

They sat there at Shea, lit only by the lights from the parking lot, sometimes going a few minutes without either one of them saying anything, because there was nothing for them to say, nothing was going to change the fact that Tim was leaving.

Will had never known his mom, so he'd never thought of her having left him the way his dad did. So there was nothing in his life that had ever made him feel as if he were being left behind, or alone.

Until now.

"I even asked my dad if I could live with you guys just until the season was over," Tim said.

"That's an *awesome* idea!" Will said. "I'm sure my dad would go for it in a heartbeat."

"Yeah, but mine didn't. He gave me his speech about family all over again."

"Dads will do that."

Tim said, "I'm gonna miss you most of all, dude."

"I never felt cheated about not having a brother because I had you," Will said.

"And that won't ever change. We can talk every night on the computer. Or do that Skype deal. And talk on Facebook as much as we want. The only thing you won't have to do is carry me in school anymore."

"Facebook friends instead of Forbes friends," Will said.

"And you can visit Arizona and I can come back here for a couple of weeks in the summer," Tim said.

Trying to find all these ways of telling Will that things weren't going to be different. Even though they both knew that things between them would never be the same.

After a while, they finally ran out of ways to lie to each other about how this wasn't such a calamity after all.

Will said, "You want to come back to my house and hang out?"

Tim said, "Maybe tomorrow; I'm pretty whipped tonight."

They walked together until they got to the corner of Knollwood, Tim's block, bumped fists and then shoulders the way they always did. Will walked the rest of the way to Valley alone, ball still under his arm. Trying to remember what he felt like when he'd taken the walk *to* Shea tonight.

Back when life was good. Before he found out that the part of Forbes, Pennsylvania, that mattered the most to him was moving away now.

His father was watching the Auburn-LSU game when Will walked through the door. He took one look at Will's face and immediately muted the sound. "What's wrong?"

"Tim's moving. His dad found a job in Arizona."

"You want to talk about it?"

"I don't even want to *think* about it," Will said.

"I know you don't want to hear this," his dad said. "But you'll get through this."

"What if I don't want to?" Will said.

"I'm here if you need me," Joe Tyler said. "You know I'm not going anywhere."

Will went upstairs, closed his door to close out the sound of the football game from downstairs. Turned on his laptop. They'd done all that talking about Facebook at Shea, so Will went to Tim's page now, even knowing exactly what it looked like, what pictures were on it, knowing how many were of the two of them, laughing their stupid heads off in just about every one of them.

They hadn't just talked about going to high school together, playing high school football together; they were already planning to go to the same college.

My best friend, Will thought.

For one more week.

Where did he write a letter to change *that*?

26

You guys know I'm not big on speeches," Will's dad said right before the Becker Falls game at Shea.

"You're joking, right, Coach?" Tim said. "You can't believe how many of your pre-game talks are on YouTube already."

Tim being Tim, to the end.

Will knew it was an act, knew how much Tim was hurting, knew how it was eating him up to be playing his last game for the Bulldogs before his farewell pizza party at their favorite restaurant, Vicolo's, tonight.

But he wasn't going to let it show.

"Very funny," Joe Tyler said.

"Keepin' it real, Mr. T.," Tim said.

Will's dad went and stood next to Tim now, put his arm around his shoulders.

"I don't even want to think about playing the rest of the season without this knucklehead," he said. "But for today, he's still a Bulldog. And we're all gonna do our best to put him on that plane with one more win."

"This is your championship game today," Will said to Tim. Then grinned and said, "So please don't you be the one who screws it up."

"Win one for me!" Tim yelled.

And yet despite that rallying cry, it was 13–0 for Becker Falls before the first quarter was even over. They took the opening kickoff and went on a long drive, using only two short passes, the rest of the time just coming right at the Bulldogs with the first option offense they'd seen all season, mixing it up with their quarterback, tailback, fullback.

They were wearing the Steelers' modern-day colors, black and gold, and this was just old-fashioned, smashmouth football. And when the Bulldogs couldn't make a first down on their first series, the Panthers got the ball back and did the same thing again.

They weren't winning one for Tim now; they were losing one. Badly. It was why they started hearing it out of the stands the way they usually did when things started to go wrong.

And, as usual, it was just one, loud, constant, unhappy voice. Dick Keenan's.

"They're doing everything except telling you the plays," he yelled. *"And you still can't stop them."*

"Toby Keenan, did you forget everything I taught you about playing linebacker?"

After another play when the quarterback faked a pitch and kept the ball for a first down, they all heard this:

"*Borrrrrrrrring.*"

When Toby finally did fight off a couple of blockers, get into the backfield and bring the tailback down for a five-yard loss, this is what passed for positive reinforcement from his dad:

"*Wait a second: You finally figured out that the game started?*"

When the Bulldogs got the ball back at 13–0, Will's dad gave Toby a couple of plays off and sent in Hannah. In the huddle Tim said, "You know what I'm not gonna miss when I get to Arizona? Listening to that guy."

Will said, "I have a feeling you'll still be able to hear him."

"Well, let's go make some first downs," Tim said, "that's the only way we can shut him up."

And they did, going on a long drive of their own, Will carrying the ball most of the time. Chris hit Tim for a big play on third-and-twelve from the Panthers' thirty-two-yard line and Will followed up by blowing through a huge hole and scoring untouched from the Panthers' twenty for the Bulldogs' first score of the game. Hannah kicked the extra point and it was 13–7. After a Panthers fumble and a couple of traded punts, it was still 13–7 at halftime.

"Listen," Joe Tyler said when he gathered them around him. "We're fine."

Fine? Will thought.

"We wouldn't be if their quarterback could throw even a lick,"

Will's dad said. "But he can't. As big as he is, he's got a rag arm. So even though we're still gonna line up the same way as always on defense, I want our cornerbacks to think of themselves as just two more outside linebackers. As soon as they snap the ball, you're selling out on the run right away. If he wants to try to beat us throwing, I say, bring it on. We're not losing to these guys, I promise."

Will said, "And we're not letting Tim go out with an *L*."

One last time, with just one half left in his football season, Tim was Tim.

"I already have enough ways to be a loser," he said.

But things didn't change at the start of the second half. The Bulldogs made a couple of first downs before getting stopped, Hannah punted, and the Panthers started in with their option running game all over again, pounding away.

So did Dick Keenan.

"You call that defense? 'Cause it's pretty offensive *to anybody who knows anything about football."*

Both the quarterback and tailback from Becker Falls were almost as big as Toby. And it seemed that every time they lined up, they were sure to get four or five or six yards. Toby was trying to disrupt them, trying to move around right up until the ball was snapped sometimes.

Nothing worked for more than one play.

With three minutes left in the third quarter, the Panthers scored another touchdown. Only a great tackle by Toby kept them from making a two-point conversion.

"A stop!" Dick Keenan yelled. *"Will wonders never cease?"*

Joe Tyler was waving his players to the sideline, telling them to hustle over before the kick. On their way, Toby said to Will, "Sorry."

"Don't you apologize," Will said. "You're playing your butt off."

"I'm talking about my dad," Toby said. "If I could play better, maybe he'd yell less."

"Don't start blaming yourself for the way he acts at games," Will said. "You're not the problem. He is. So don't think about him." He pointed to where the Panthers were getting ready to kick. "Think about the two scores we're gonna put on them between now and the end of this game."

Will's dad knelt down in the middle of the circle, telling them they were going to go to a no-huddle offense on the next series, telling Chris the first three plays they were going to run.

"There's still plenty of time," Joe Tyler said. "But let's speed things up, anyway."

They did. Pass to Will in the flat, pass to Hannah on the sideline, a screen for Toby that Will's dad had drawn up at halftime and went for twenty yards. On the last play of the third quarter, Will seemed to have gotten stopped on the goal line, told himself to keep his legs moving, fell into the end zone.

It was 19–14 now at Shea, one quarter to go, in a game they couldn't afford to lose.

Because the Bulldogs only had twelve players, Will noticed that the refs would give them a longer break every chance they got, on changes of possession or the ends of quarters. By now, Joe Tyler knew to expect it, so he had the players come to the sideline again, get some water or Gatorade.

As they did, he went up to every one of them, either slapping them on the pads or helmet, stopping to hug Tim, and then Will.

"We're doing this," Will's dad said.

Will nodded.

But right then, as if on cue, they heard Dick Keenan. Will noticed that the longer the game went on, the more the yelling was directed at all of them, Will's dad included, and not just Toby.

"While you're hugging it out with them, maybe you could tell them to tackle somebody."

Joe Tyler turned toward the bleachers now and said, "That's it."

Turned back toward the field, waved the ref over, asked if he could call a time-out even if they were basically in a long time-out already.

"What's up, Joe?" the ref said.

Will's dad said, "I need a minute to shut somebody up."

The ref said, "The guy at the top of the bleachers with the leather lungs?"

"Him."

"Be my guest." With that he blew his whistle, extended his arms in the direction of both benches, said, "Official time-out."

As soon as he did, Joe Tyler walked over to the bleachers behind the Bulldogs' bench, yelled up to Dick Keenan, "Hey, Dick, come down here; there's something I need to tell you."

In that moment, it was as if all sound completely disappeared from Shea Field.

Will watched Toby's dad, arms crossed in front of him, face clenched like always, staring down at Joe Tyler.

"Just coach your team," he said.

"Trying," Joe Tyler said. "But you won't let me."

"Free country."

Will stood and watched it all, heart pounding. He wondered what the Becker Falls kids, their coach, thought was happening over here. Not knowing that this was the real action now at Shea, before the fourth quarter even started.

"Oh, I know it's a free country," Joe Tyler said. "And that means free speech, too. Just come down here for a second. I'm not like you." Will could see his dad grinning. "I don't want everybody to hear."

It was as if he'd challenged him, in this easygoing way. And left Toby's dad no choice. He walked down through the bleachers now, the other parents giving him plenty of room, staring at Joe Tyler the whole time, looking the way he always did, like he spent his whole life being mad at the world.

Then the only thing separating Will's dad and Toby's dad was the fence.

This is it, Will thought.

This is what we've been waiting for, somebody to tell this guy off.

Will stole a look at Toby, who'd taken his helmet off, was just watching the scene play out the way everybody else was.

How long had Toby been waiting for somebody to tell off his dad?

Dick Keenan spoke first.

Of course.

"There's a game going on," he said. "Not that the guys on your defense seem to have noticed."

Now, Will thought.

Now.

"You noticed, huh?" Joe Tyler said, surprising Will, still keeping his cool.

"Your kids, starting with *my* kid, couldn't stop a nosebleed today," Dick Keenan said.

"You're right."

He still had his arms crossed in front of him, still looked as if he would come right over the fence if Will's dad said the wrong thing.

But now he looked confused, as if Will's dad were trying to trick him somehow.

"I'm . . . right?"

"It's why I called you down," Joe Tyler said. "I said I wanted to tell you something. But the truth is, I wanted to *ask* you something."

"Well, hurry up, before they flag you for delay of game."

"You still think you know everything about defense, right?"

"More than you, that's for sure."

"Then here's my question: why don't you come over here and help me try to win this game?"

And to everybody's amazement, starting with Toby, that is exactly what Dick Keenan did.

27

As soon as Toby had brought down the Becker Falls kick returner at the thirty-yard line, Joe Tyler signaled to the ref for a real time-out, waved the Bulldogs over to the sideline all over again.

And once they were in the huddle around Dick Keenan, they found out that when you could get him to stop acting like a blowhard—or a bully—even for a couple of minutes, he actually knew what he was talking about.

It was almost like he'd been waiting for somebody to give him the chance to prove it.

It wasn't like he turned into a good guy all of a sudden, or got better at talking to guys their age, or even acted like a good dad. But he knew his football; you could hear that right away. Especially defensive football.

When he started talking too loudly, Joe Tyler said in a much calmer voice, "Dick, we can hear you fine." He nodded at the Panthers. "We just don't want them to hear, too."

Will saw something pass across Dick Keenan's face for a second, a look that he was sure Toby knew like his own name, but then it was gone.

He said to the Bulldogs: "Listen up, we got about a minute to put in a defense. We used to call it the '50' when Joe and me played. This won't be that. But we're gonna put five in the box, put four backers behind 'em. Leaving us with two cover corners, no safety."

He pointed at Johnny and Hannah, the two corners. "You get up on their receivers, because there's no chance that kid can throw deep with that wet noodle arm of his. And give run support whenever you can. Got it?"

They all nodded.

Dick Keenan said to Toby, "You spy on the quarterback. The two linebackers on the outside"—he pointed at Tim and Gerry Dennis—"you do *not* let the stinkin' ball get to the outside one more time today. You git it?"

Tim and Gerry nodded, like they were afraid not to.

They all heard the whistle now. Will turned and saw the ref walking slowly toward them, like a baseball umpire ready to break up a conference on the mound.

"You follow the ball," Dick Keenan said, "not where you think it might end up." He was kneeling. Now he looked up at them. "Any questions?" Nobody said anything. "This ain't rocket science. It's about who wants it more. If you do, now would be a good time to show it."

Joe Tyler had told Will that Dick Keenan was always the quar-

terback of the Forbes High defense when they were teammates.
Now that became Toby's job. Somehow he was playing even harder
now than before, which was saying plenty. Like there was a chance
for him to do something more than beat Becker Falls today.

Dick Keenan's defense started working right away. On first
down, the Panthers' quarterback faked the pitch to the tailback,
but Toby didn't bite, planted the quarterback instead for a three-
yard loss. On second down the tailback got the ball, looking like
he could get to the edge the way he had all day. But Tim beat him
to his spot, forced him to the inside. Toby was waiting for him.
The kid was lucky to hold on to the ball.

No gain.

The quarterback did try to throw on third-and-long, rolling to
his right, but Jeremiah Keating read the play perfectly, dropped
back on the tight end, knocked the ball down.

Three and out. The Panthers brought in their punter. Will and
Tim dropped back, Tim just there to block. Will looked over at
their sideline. Dick Keenan still had his arms crossed in front of
him. But something about his face had changed now. He didn't
look happy. Will wondered if anything made this guy happy. But
there was definitely something different.

Will thought: *He's like my dad.*

He's back on the field finally and he likes it.

Will got off a good return, taking the ball back to midfield.
Chris faked it to Will on first down, straightened up, hit Toby for
six yards. But then Will got caught in the backfield for a five-yard
loss, only got eight on third down.

They had to punt now, Will worrying as they did that they might have handed momentum right back to the Panthers. Only they hadn't. Because they weren't beating the Bulldogs with the option anymore, couldn't solve the new defensive formation, mostly couldn't get through or around Toby Keenan, who played like he was on some kind of mission now. He made all three tackles on the Panthers' next series, forced them to punt again.

Still 19–14. Four minutes left now. Bulldogs' ball on their forty.

Right before Chris called the first-down play in the huddle, a 38 Toss to Will, Tim put his hands on Will's shoulders and said, "Thrill? You think you could win this sucker for me?"

"We all can," Will said.

And then gained twenty yards on 38 Toss. From their forty to the Becker Falls forty, just like that. Chris handed it to Will now on a counter-play. He gained eight more yards. Then four more on a direct-snap Wildcat play his dad had installed for today's game. Another first down. Ball moving, chains moving. The Panthers had called two of their time-outs already. They had one left.

Tim pointed that out in the huddle.

"They can stop the clock one more time," Will said. "Just not us."

They ran 38 Toss again, and it was as if the Panthers hadn't seen it all day. This time Will took it all the way to their fourteen.

Minute and a half left.

Now the Panthers called their last time-out.

It was all Will Tyler now. He knew it; the Panthers knew it. He carried up the middle for six yards, then ran off-tackle for four more. First-and-goal. He could have gotten a yard or two more but had no chance to get into the end zone. Decided to stay inbounds. Let the clock run.

Will tried to run left on first down but slipped as he made his cut, went down for a two-yard loss. Got back to the four on second, before getting stuffed by their nose tackle.

Third down from the four. Fifteen seconds now. Will's dad had two time-outs left, called one of them now. Signaled for the play he wanted.

35 Dive, to Will.

In the huddle Will said to Chris, "I'll line up at fullback. Give the ball to Tim."

There was a long pause and Chris said, "You sure?"

Will said, "I'm so sure you wouldn't believe it."

"You don't have to do this," Tim said.

"Yeah," Will said. "I sort of do."

Chris went on a short count, taking the snap from Wes as Ernie Accorsi tried to push the Panthers' nose tackle all the way out of the back of the end zone. When the middle linebacker tried to step up and fill the hole, Will took him down with the hardest block he'd ever thrown in his life, sealing the hole for the friend who had sealed so many for him.

Tim LeBlanc scored standing up. His final touchdown as a Bulldog.

Bulldogs 20, Panthers 19. The refs didn't even bother having Hannah come out to kick the point. Game over.

When Tim broke free, Will handed him the ball.

"This belongs to you," he said.

Tim said, "I didn't know we could keep game balls."

Joe Tyler was there now. "You can carry that baby all the way to Arizona."

Then the Bulldogs were swarming Tim again. When they finally settled down, on their way to get the snacks Ernie's mom had brought today, Will watched Toby break off on his own and start walking toward his dad.

Dick Keenan watched him come, no smile on him, no change of expression. When Toby got close enough, all his dad did was nod slightly, then point at his son.

A start, Will thought.

This time Toby didn't have to walk to the parking lot alone.

Will and Tim decided to say their good-byes in front of Vicolo's when Tim's party was over.

Will's dad and Tim's parents were the last ones left inside, finishing their coffee. Now it was just Will and Tim on Main Street, neither one of them wanting to act as if they were actually *saying* good-bye to each other.

Tim kept saying he'd call Will tomorrow as soon as he got to Scottsdale.

"I keep thinking that because of the time change, you'll get scores before I will," Tim said.

Will said, "You would think that."

"The only thing I really know about the Arizona Cardinals," Tim said, "is that we beat them that time in the Super Bowl."

We. The Steelers.

"That's the way we're probably gonna beat Castle Rock," Tim said. "Some last-second hero play."

We. The Bulldogs.

"That," Will said, "would be sweet."

"Don't *you* screw it up for *me*," Tim said. "You know how the story is supposed to end."

"Tell me about it."

All their lives they'd been able to read each other's minds, know what the other one was going to say before he said it. And now it was as if they were just trying to find things to talk about.

"You're sure New Balance won't care that I'm keeping all my equipment?"

"My dad talked to them," Will said. "Mr. DeMartini said that everybody gets to keep their stuff when the season's over. Especially one of the original eleven."

"Back down to eleven."

"Nah, we're still twelve," Will said. "We've just got one of our best subs in Arizona now."

"Dude," Tim said, "you gotta go all the way."

Just like that, it was *you*. Maybe it was as good a way for Tim to say good-bye as any.

They bumped fists, then shoulders with a quick lean-in. No hug.

"Have a good trip," Will said.

"Probably sleep all the way," Tim said.

"With that game ball on the seat next to you."

"You know it."

Tim's parents came outside. Will shook hands with Mr. Le-Blanc. Mrs. LeBlanc was a hugger, holding on to Will longer than he would have hoped before she finally pulled back. Nothing more to do or say. Will stood there watching them walk to the corner of Elm, where they'd parked their car.

Before Tim got in, he turned and shouted down the block to Will.

"Promise me you're gonna beat those guys."

"Promise," Will said. "And you know how I am with promises."

Then Tim got into the car and it made the turn on Elm and was gone.

One of the original eleven in that car.

One Will missed already.

Three games left in the regular season: Camden, LaGrange, Morganville.

No margin for error, in any way. The Bulldogs still had to win out to lock down their spot in the championship game. And they had to stay healthy. They had no chance to write the ending they all wanted with ten players. Simple as that, and not just simple math.

Three games left, two at home, the last two. Win them all and they were playing Castle Rock at Shea the week after the Morganville game.

But now it was the Friday before they were going on the road to play in Camden, and Will and Hannah were having lunch in the cafeteria, the usual Friday mac-and-cheese, Hannah having already scarfed hers and finished half of Will's. It was nothing either one of them had talked about, but they'd been having lunch together every day at school since Tim had left.

"You know, I wasn't going to mention this," she said, "but I think I might have broken my index finger when I made that tackle at the end of practice last night."

"*What?*"

He turned and saw the smile and knew right away that he'd been punked.

"Not funny," he said.

"Kind of funny."

"Then how come I'm not laughing?"

"Oh, come on, I was just *joking*. If Tim had said something like that, you would've thought it was funny, admit it."

"Listen," Will said. "I've tried to explain this to you before. I *get* that you're funny. I just don't always *think* you're funny."

"You gotta chill, Thrill. Nobody's gotten hurt so far. Why do you keep thinking something bad is gonna happen every time the ball is snapped?"

She asked if he wanted his brownie and he told her to have it, he wasn't that hungry.

Will said, "It's just because we're so close."

"So stop worrying!" she said. "You're not even good at being a worrier, so don't even try, you idiot. You always believe things are gonna work out great. Maybe that's why for you they usually do."

"Not always."

"Most ways."

"Tim left."

"Yeah," she said, "he did. So things don't always go perfectly for you. But they're not so terrible, either. Now we've even got the meanest guy in town not only acting like a good guy, but a good coach."

Dick Keenan hadn't dialed himself down completely. But at least now he was barking out instructions at practice, teaching them new formations on the fly, even having Toby call out defensive signals now the way Dick Keenan had done when he was the middle linebacker at Forbes High.

So practices had gotten much louder, no doubt. Toby's dad was tougher on them than Will's dad was. *Much.* And occasionally, right in front of the players, Joe Tyler would find a way to tell Mr. Keenan to lower his voice, joking that there were laws in Forbes about making too much noise in public places.

Even Toby wasn't afraid now to tell his dad to cool it once in a while. He'd done that the night before, after his dad had gotten all over Johnny Callahan for missing a tackle.

Dick Keenan, red-faced, had said, "I just want you guys to get it."

"*We* get that, Dad," Toby said in a quiet voice. "Trust me. We *all* get that."

Will had watched the two of them, holding his breath. But one more time Toby's dad surprised him and let it go.

For all three practices this week, including one he'd run himself because one of Joe Tyler's classes got moved up a night, he'd brought one new defense with him, walking them through it, running from one spot to another, telling them what they were supposed to do if an offensive guy blocked down this way, or the quarterback rolled out that way, or the receivers crossed and tried to pick off defenders.

When practice was over that night, he'd said, "Playing defense the way you were before, I swear, I don't know how you beat anybody."

When he was out of earshot, Will turned to Chris Aiello and said, "My dad says Mr. Keenan is still kind of a work in progress."

After school on Friday, Will walked home alone. He was getting used to it already, not having Tim at his side, not having Tim talk and talk all the way to his house, or Will's, acting as if every single thing that had happened to him at school was totally fascinating to Will. Hannah couldn't pick up the slack here, the way she did at lunch, because she was staying after school most days now to work on the school paper she and a couple of other kids were trying to start up.

"Hey," she'd said, "it's the family business."

So Will was alone on the walk home the way he was alone in the house until his dad showed up from work.

Today he decided to take a slight detour, to one of his favorite spots along the river, finding his favorite rock, throwing down his backpack, pulling out a bottle of Castle Rock water, staring across at what he'd spent most of his life thinking was a better place to live.

Only he didn't feel that way anymore.

He was happy now on this side of the river. He would have

been a lot happier if his best friend hadn't left here. But he didn't want to be *there* anymore. He wanted to be here. With the Bull-dogs. Even with Hannah Grayson. He wanted to be on the team that beat Ben Clark's team, and Kendrick's, the team that didn't have to worry about their cool uniforms or their cool turf field.

He wanted to do it on this side of the river.

Hannah talked about how he believed that things were al-ways going to work out great. But in his heart, he wasn't so sure at the start of the season, wasn't sure their eleven—the only eleven they had—could beat Castle Rock's.

But now, even back to eleven, Will believed they could.

He kept trying not to get ahead of himself, not with three games left, even if only one of the teams—Morganville—had a winning record. But sometimes he couldn't help it.

Today he told himself to chill, the way Hannah had told him to, enjoy a view from this spot that looked a whole lot different to him than it had six weeks ago.

He heard the brief blast of a car horn then, turned around, saw that it was his dad's white-and-blue USPS truck. Saw his dad waving to him through the open window. Saw him park at the top of the hill, get out and bend his knee a couple of times. One thing hadn't changed with Joe Tyler, even with things going good with their team:

He still had a real bad knee.

He kept telling Will that he felt no pain these days. But his son knew better.

"When you weren't at home, I thought I might find you here," his dad said, making his way carefully down the bank. "Want some company?"

"Always."

There was enough room for both of them on the flat, smooth rock. His dad sat down, stretching the bad leg in front of him, kneading it with his big right hand. Will offered him some water and he drank some. Then they just sat there in silence for a few minutes, watching the water move past them, on its way to meeting up downriver with the Ohio. Joe Tyler, Will knew from experience, wasn't his buddy Tim. He never talked just to talk.

After a while he said, "I just wanted to thank you, pal."

Will turned, saw his dad was still staring out at the water.

"Thank me for what?"

His dad said, "For getting me to coach."

"You're thanking *me*? Dad, we would've had no chance without *you*. Are you insane? You're the best coach I've ever played for. That *any* of us have ever played for."

"Doesn't happen without you," Joe Tyler said.

Maybe it was just the day for it, Will getting credit for stuff he didn't think he had anything to do with.

"You sound like Hannah."

"I'm just gonna hope that's a good thing."

"Don't tell her. But it is."

Joe Tyler said, "There's a line my old high school coach used to use on us all the time. He said great coaches are the ones who take their belief in their players and get the players to believe in themselves."

"That's what you've done with us."

"No, see, that's the thing," his dad said. "It's different with us. It took you believing in *me* to get me believing in all of *you.*"

"I just asked you to do something I wanted you to do, and I thought you wanted to do," Will said. "And something we could do together."

"Doing this together, like this, it's made me love football again," Joe Tyler said.

"I can see that, Dad. I think everybody on the team can."

"But here's the thing, pal: I never thought it could happen. I didn't just stop loving football; I blamed it for just about every bad thing that ever happened to me, with the exception of your mom passing. I blamed it for a lot of pain, pal, and not just in my knee." He nodded. "So thanks for a lot of stuff."

"You're welcome," Will said.

They sat there for what felt like a long time after that, just the two of them, watching as a sleek-looking motorboat roared past them. Then they were talking about the first ten plays Joe Tyler wanted to run against Camden tomorrow on the road, both of them getting excited.

Yeah, Will thought.

Yeah, man.

This side of the river was *exactly* where he belonged at that moment, exactly where he wanted to be.

29

They beat Camden, 20–0, Hannah scoring her second touchdown of the season on a play Joe Tyler had drawn up on the sideline before they ran it, Will looking as if he were running 38 Toss to the right, then pulling up and throwing a pass to where Hannah was standing wide open between the goalposts.

"Finally," she said before she kicked the point. "You identify the best receiver on the team."

"It would have been, like, criminal not to," Will said.

"Tell me about it."

A good day all around, starting with the fact that they made it through another week without anybody getting hurt. And the gadget play to start the game, the flea flicker to Toby, went for sixty yards and a touchdown, the Bulldogs never looking back from there.

So their record was 4–2. Two wins away from the rematch with the Castle Rock Bears, who just kept winning themselves, still undefeated, the only close call they'd had all season coming against the Bulldogs.

It was the game Will thought about all the time, not just because he'd come up a yard short, but because they'd come that close without Toby.

Without a difference maker like Toby.

And Will had to admit that they'd come as close as they had to upsetting the Bears without Mr. Keenan being in charge of the defense.

"He's like our Dick LeBeau," Jeremiah said at practice one night. "Just much louder and much meaner."

Talking about the Steelers' Hall of Fame defensive coordinator.

And Will had said, "Mr. Keenan probably thinks Dick LeBeau doesn't know anything about defense, either."

Will could never see himself warming up to the guy, even if he did seem to be working on keeping his temper—and mouth— under control. But there was no getting around the fact that Toby's dad was as much a reason for the shutout at Camden as anybody else. And why the Bulldogs held LaGrange to just one touchdown the next Saturday in a 14–6 win at Shea.

The LaGrange Jaguars only had one win on the season coming into the game but played out of their minds, especially on defense, and had a chance to score and maybe tie the game with a two-point conversion in the last minute before Toby stepped up and just crushed their tailback on a fourth-and-one from the Bulldogs' five-yard line.

When it was over, Will asked his dad if he could give Mr. Keenan the game ball. Joe Tyler said, have it. But Mr. Keenan shook his head, wouldn't even put his hands on the ball.

"Players win games," he said, "not coaches. Always have, always will." He gave a nod to Toby. "You want to give it to somebody so bad, give it to him."

Will did that as Mr. Keenan walked away.

Joe Tyler leaned down and whispered to Will, "*Still* a work in progress."

"Little like our team," Will said.

"Which still has a lot of work left," his dad said.

He was talking about the game against Morganville next Saturday, which was the same as a conference championship game that could put you in the Super Bowl.

Win and they were in the West River league version of the Super Bowl.

When they got back to Forbes, Will and his dad went for pizza at Vicolo's. On the way home, Mr. Tyler said he wanted to take a slight detour, backtracking to the middle of town, to the park known as McElroy Square, across the street from the Forbes Flyers factory.

Will assumed there was a reason for this; his dad hardly ever did anything without a reason. Without some kind of point he wanted to make. When he shut off the car, on the McElroy Square side of the street, Will just waited to find out what it was this time.

"There was a time," Joe Tyler said finally, "when this part of Forbes didn't just feel like the center of town, it felt like the center of my world."

He hit a button on the side of the seat, pushing the driver's seat back as far as he could so he could stretch his bad leg a little.

"Forbes really was a pretty happening place once," he said. "Until it wasn't."

Will knew that, of course. Knew the story. But his dad's own story was part of it, and that's why Will never got tired of listening to it.

"I hated watching that factory go belly-up, and the town nearly going belly-up along with it," Joe Tyler said in a soft voice. "But the truth was, I hated that factory long before that. Hated that I had to go work in it when I came back after I messed up college. Because that factory—in my mind, anyway—meant that I was a failure. I hadn't turned out to be the football player I wanted to be. Worse than that? I hadn't turned out to be the *person* I wanted to be. I'd go into that factory long before it ever closed and think that I was the one who'd gone belly-up."

Will just sat there, slightly turned in his seat, watching his dad's face, the windows down, the park empty, the sidewalks empty in this part of Forbes that was once the center of everything.

Will had never heard his dad tell it like this before.

Joe Tyler turned now.

"This making any sense to you?"

"A lot."

"Liar."

Will smiled and said, "Now you really do sound like Hannah." His dad smiled back.

"You know," Joe Tyler said, "when I was playing on the high school team, when we won the state title the year before I got hurt, they started having pep rallies in the Square on Friday nights. The factory would keep all its lights on and there'd always be this huge 'Go Falcons' banner stretched outside the top two floors. And it would seem as if half the town, or even more, came out to cheer us on."

Joe Tyler paused and said, "We used to think Coach Carson gave better pre-game speeches to the crowd on Friday nights than he did us on Saturday afternoon. Now he's retiring after the season, Coach is, he announced that the other day. One more part of my life that will be gone."

"Those pep rallies sound like something out of *Friday Night Lights*," Will said.

"I never thought of it that way, but yeah, it was." He was smiling again. "We made some noise in those days."

Will said, "I'll bet."

His dad turned to him, eyes bright. "Let's make some of our own now," he said. "Let's us make some noise in this old town, so people know *it* hasn't closed up. Or given up."

"Sounds like a plan to me," Will said to his dad.

Then his dad started up the car and pulled away from McElroy

Square, Will thinking that his dad had started out telling his own story tonight and then it had changed.

Into *their* story.

His and Will's.

"Everybody around here has been down a long time," Joe Tyler said as he made the turn past Shea toward Valley Road. "Let's see if we can make them stand up and cheer."

30

They fell behind early against Morganville, which turned out to be as big a team, size-wise, as they had faced all year, especially in the offensive and defensive lines.

It made Will think of one of Tim's favorite lines when they'd go up against much bigger players, in any sport:

"I think my dad went to college with some of those guys."

Funny how often Tim's voice was still inside his head, even when they weren't talking every night on the phone, or on the computer, or Facebook.

But Tim wasn't going to help them beat Morganville's Jaguars today. Tim was in Arizona and Will and the other Bulldogs were behind 9–0 at the start of the second quarter. The Jaguars had scored a touchdown on their second drive of the game, then got a safety a few minutes later, Hannah trying to punt out of their end zone, and Wes's long snap nearly going through the uprights.

It looked as if the Bulldogs were finally going to score on their last drive of the half, their best drive of the game so far. But on third-and-eight from the Jaguars' twenty, Chris threw one behind Toby on a crossing pattern, the ball bounced off Toby's back shoulder, went straight into the air, came down into the waiting arms of the free safety.

Half over. Jaguars still leading, 9–0.

The game had started later than usual, three o'clock. By then, all of the Bulldogs knew that Becker Falls had already won its game against Merrell. So if the Bulldogs didn't come back in the second half, it would be Becker Falls hosting the championship game next Saturday.

Totally unacceptable.

Will's dad didn't make any rousing speech at halftime, didn't even act as if they were behind. Or that their season might have just one half left to it. He just gathered them around him and told them that once they received the second-half kickoff, they were going to run the stinking ball right down the Jaguars' throats. Show them that the only thing making them tired was losing the battle at the line of scrimmage, that even though the Bulldogs were smaller, they were going to beat them with smash-mouth football.

When he finished, he looked right at Will. "I'm gonna be asking a lot of you in the second half," he said.

"Wouldn't want it any other way," he said.

Chris Aiello gave Will a playful shove. "You got us into this," Chris said. "Now you get us out of it."

They ran the ball ten times on the drive that took up most of
the third quarter. Other than a quarterback sneak from Chris on
a third-and-one play and one cool inside reverse to Toby, Will
carried the ball on eight of those plays.

The last one was from the Morganville seven-yard line. Will
got jammed up trying to go off-tackle, bounced the play to the
outside. Ended up one-on-one in the open field with one of the
Morganville linebackers.

It was just big fun from there.

For Will, not the linebacker.

Will had been running hard to his right trying to get to the
edge and around the corner. But now he planted his left foot,
nearly coming to a dead stop, even switched the ball to his left
hand to sell the fake a little more. The backer went for it, squared
his shoulders and lowered them, going for Will's legs, wanting
to wrap him up.

And tackled nothing but air.

Will had made one of those cuts he could make on the fly, to
the right sideline, the kind of cut you had to be born being able
to make. There and gone. Completely dusted the kid, didn't even
bother switching the ball back, could have walked into the end
zone. Lined up in the slot while Hannah kicked the extra point.

It was 9–7 now.

Game on.

The Jaguars didn't stop playing just because Will had his team
on the board. They drove down the field, deep into Bulldogs' ter-

ritory, before Toby forced their quarterback to fumble on a blind-side blitz Dick Keenan had called out to Toby right before the snap.

So now the Bulldogs were driving again—before they were the ones turning the ball over—Johnny Callahan making a great catch on a deep post but getting pancaked between two defenders and coughing up the ball, slamming the grass hard in frustration after he did.

Here came the Jaguars again in the fourth quarter, keeping the ball on the ground themselves, starting to wear down the Bulldogs for real. Finally ending up with a third-and-goal from the five-yard line. Not wanting to take any chances, they tried to run a simple sweep for their tailback, but there was Toby again, exploding the blocking in front of him, dropping the kid in his tracks for a three-yard loss.

Fourth-and-goal from the eight. Will knew they weren't trying a field goal; the kid kicking off for them couldn't even make the ball go thirty yards. But a touchdown here for the Jaguars made it a two-score game, with four minutes left. A stop here and the Bulldogs still had to go ninety-five yards to win the game.

The Jaguars tried to throw the ball in Hannah's direction, to the wide receiver on her side. Throw it up and let their kid go up and get it. But the quarterback didn't get enough air under the ball, and Hannah timed her jump perfectly and broke it up.

She didn't celebrate when the ball ended up on the ground or act surprised that she'd made the play.

Just turned and pointed at Will.

As if to say: Told you so.

It wasn't a two-score game. Still just one.

Go the length of the field and get one more touchdown and get their shot at Castle Rock next Saturday.

It's like they always told you, Will thought:

Go big or go home.

In the huddle Will said to his teammates, "We didn't come all this way to lose."

Will took his stance behind Chris, thinking about how all along Hannah had been saying it was his team. If she was right, it had to be his team now.

On first down he took a simple 34 Dive and ran twenty yards with it, their free safety lucky to trip him up with a diving tackle from the side. Then they ran a play called Sweep 7, the "7" meaning to his left. He got ten yards. Then they ran it to the other side, Sweep 8, and Will got fifteen more.

Just like that, they were on the Morganville side of midfield.

Less than two minutes left.

Chris hit Toby on a fifteen-yard buttonhook, then handed off to Will on a counter that went for nine more. Now they were at Morganville's twenty-six-yard line. One minute left. The Morganville coach called one of the two time-outs he had left, stopping the clock.

Joe Tyler called for another counter to Will, who saw his

blocking take shape and blew through the hole all the way to the Morganville fifteen. Now it was his dad's turn to call a time-out.

Thirty seconds left at Shea.

On the next play, what was going to be a 38 Toss to Will, Chris got anxious and pulled away from center too quickly, dropping the ball. Like he was putting their whole season on the ground.

Fortunately Jeremiah Keating was there to fall on it. Joe Tyler called the second of his three time-outs.

Seventeen seconds left.

Second-and-twelve.

Chris gathered himself and threw a short, safe pass to Will in the flat. Will managed to turn up the field and get to the four-yard line before getting knocked out-of-bounds.

First-and-goal from there.

Eight seconds left.

Will figured they had two shots from here, even with one time-out still in his dad's pocket.

"38 Toss," Chris said in the huddle.

Another pitch to Will. Get to the end zone or get out-of-bounds behind all the blockers he usually had on one of their go-to plays, a sweep to the right.

On their way out of the huddle Chris leaned over to Will, like he was giving him last-minute instructions. But he really wasn't.

"Thrill, the only block you're gonna need on this sucker is *mine.*"

Chris took the snap, turned and pitched the ball, busted it getting out in front of Will. Will watched him go low and hard into the Jaguars' middle linebacker. Toby Keenan cleared out everybody else, made the rest of the defense look like bowling pins scattering. Will took a hard hit at the one from somebody. But Troy Polamalu and James Harrison weren't going to stop him getting in from there. Neither was the old Steel Curtain defense. Will got knocked sideways a little, but when he came down, he saw that his whole body was across the new chalk goal line at Shea.

Bulldogs 13, Jaguars 9, only zeros showing on the clock.

Toby got to Will first, lifting him up in the air as easily as he would have a baby, spinning him around.

It was when Will was facing the field again that he saw that Chris Aiello was still sitting at the three-yard line, his right leg stretched out in front of him.

"Dude, put me down!" Will said to Toby.

"Sorry. Got carried away."

"No," Will said. "Something happened to Aiello."

"Yeah," Toby said. "The best block of his life, that's what happened."

"No," Will said. "I think he's hurt."

They both ran to Chris. So did the rest of the Bulldogs. Chris had his helmet off, his face contorted with pain, eyes red. He was trying to catch his breath, or maybe just trying not to cry in front of his teammates. Will's dad and Mrs. Accorsi, the team's medical trainer, were with him now.

When Mrs. Accorsi saw the angle of Chris's leg, she told him not to move it.

When Chris spoke, it was to Will, almost as if he were apologizing for something.

"I think I broke my ankle," he said.

Eventually Will's dad and Toby's dad got Chris's arms around their shoulders, helped him to his feet, Chris keeping his right leg off the ground as they walked him to the parking lot, the Bulldogs walking behind, Mrs. Accorsi telling them they were taking Chris straight to the hospital.

It wouldn't be official until his doctor looked at the X-ray an hour later. But he'd broken a bone in his right ankle.

Just like that, they were ten.

31

At Monday night's practice, Joe Tyler wouldn't allow any of his players to start feeling sorry for themselves.

"The only one we feel bad for here is Chris," he said to the team. "He's the one who lost his season here. And believe me, I know what that's like. You know that line people use, about feeling somebody's pain? Well, in this case, I can feel his."

The players were kneeling along the forty-yard line closest to Arch Street. Toby's dad was standing behind Will's dad, holding an old-fashioned black-and-white school notebook in his hand. When Will had asked him what was inside the notebook, Mr. Keenan had said, "Blitzes, for the first ten-man defense in history. Because defense still wins."

But for now he listened to Joe Tyler along with the rest of them.

"Chris lost his season, but we didn't lose ours," Will's dad said. "We've got one more game left to play. You know what old guys like Dick and I would give to have one more game like this? Anything."

He turned and said, "Am I right?"

Dick Keenan said, "I ran into Coach Carson, who used to coach Joe and me, the other day. The old man is retiring at the end of the year. He asked me how I liked coaching. Wanted to know if it was anywhere near as good as playing. Good thing I'm not still playing for him, because I said, 'Coach, all due respect, but you must be losin' your mind. *Nothing* is better than playing.'"

"Coach Keenan is right," Will's dad said. "There's nothing better than playing a game like this, against who we're playing it. On our field, in front of our fans. So the Bulldogs are underdogs again. So big deal. Been there, done that. It's like Will says: Wouldn't want it any other way."

It sounded like he was finished. They all started to get to their feet. But there was one more thing he wanted to tell them.

"We're not winning this game for Chris on Saturday. We're winning it for *us*. And for every other team that ever got told it wasn't good enough. All the other teams who had that chip on their shoulders that we got."

He put his hand out. "Now bring it in," he said.

They did. Put their hands on top of his. Then it was just left to Will to put an exclamation point to the longest speech he'd ever heard from his dad.

"Bulldogs," Will said.

The rest of the Bulldogs shouted it back at him, louder than they ever had before.

Before Dick Keenan could show off his ten-man defense, all the fancy blitzes he *had* come up with for them and for Castle Rock, there was a much bigger job, especially on the Monday night before the championship game:

They had to officially name a quarterback to replace Chris Aiello.

They had started out losing last year's quarterback and now they had lost this year's quarterback. On Sunday, Will and his dad had gone over every possible replacement for Chris, including Will.

They had finally come up with what they thought were their two best candidates: Jeremiah Keating and Johnny Callahan. Jeremiah had been the backup quarterback on the sixth-grade team last year. Johnny had never played quarterback in his life but had shown off a pretty decent arm as his Little League team's best pitcher.

Problem was, they both looked like scrubs at practice tonight.

Whatever Jeremiah had once known about the basics—taking the snap from center, pivoting smoothly and handing the ball off—he had totally forgotten. Gone. Without any defensive pressure, any pressure of any kind, he was messing up the transfer of the ball to Will about half the time. And the harder he tried to get it right, the worse things got for him. It turned out he could throw just fine, but the Bulldogs weren't a throwing team first, they were a running team.

Johnny was a little better getting the ball into Will's belly, but not much. And *his* throwing when he dropped back in the pocket was pretty much a horror. Will thought he was the one more likely to get better with time.

They just didn't *have* time.

Playing without a quarterback was as bad as playing *with* ten.

At one point, while everybody else was taking a quick water break, Will stayed on the field with his dad and Mr. Keenan.

Joe Tyler said, "We could alternate them. Jeremiah throws it better, and Johnny can at least execute a simple handoff."

"Yeah," Dick Keenan said. "And the Castle Rock coaches will barely notice that we got one guy in there to hand it off and the other guy in to throw."

They decided to go with Johnny, who promised everybody his throwing would get better in the three more practices they had between now and Saturday.

"Look at it this way, Coach," Johnny said. "No way my throwing can get any worse in that time."

They worked on defense for the rest of practice, trying to learn the blitzes Mr. Keenan had in that notebook of his, ones that he said were designed to keep Ben Clark guessing before every single snap.

"They're gonna know they're on the power play," Mr. Keenan

said at one point. "But we're gonna make 'em wonder why it don't feel like one."

Another time he said, "The whole point of this is to have enough moving parts that they don't get to exploit the fact that we happen to have a part missing."

"And a few screws loose," Joe Tyler said.

"That too," Dick Keenan said. Will thought for a second he might even get crazy on them and smile.

But he kept himself under control.

At the very end of practice, darkness coming fast now, Will's dad had them work on punting, worried that being short one blocker might get a punt blocked on Hannah in a big moment on Saturday.

So he moved a couple of guys around, put three up-backs in the backfield to block for her instead of the usual two, told the outside guys it was their job to protect the wings and give her time.

They practiced by having Wes long-snap the ball to Hannah with just three guys in front of her and everybody else— including Joe Tyler and Dick Keenan—coming at her on an all-out blitz.

They didn't block one on her. On her last kick of the night, she totally showed off, saying she was going to try to kick one out-of-bounds but just bombing one out of the back of the end zone instead, as if she wanted to remind everybody of the leg that got her on the team in the first place.

Then she was telling her teammates that she kicked that ball the way they were going to kick Kendrick and his friends all over the field on Saturday, and then the practice that had started with them thinking about the loss of their quarterback had turned into all this trash talk and laughter.

Will took off his helmet, broke off from the rest of the Bulldogs, started jogging toward the sideline.

That was when he got hit for the second time this season by a flying football that came at him out of nowhere.

This time he went down.

"What the . . . ?" he said, his head ringing, jumping up to see where the ball had come from.

It had come from Toby.

Will remembered him running off to retrieve the ball Hannah had just punted out of sight. Now he was standing in the distance, between the goalposts.

More than fifty yards away.

"I am *so* sorry!" he yelled to Will.

Running hard toward Will now, trying to explain as he did, saying, "Are you okay? I was just throwing it up there for fun, and then you ran right into it, and you didn't hear me when I yelled for you to look out."

All of a sudden, Will's head didn't hurt nearly as much as it had a few seconds ago.

"Did you say you *threw* it?"

"Yeah."

"From the back of the *end* zone?"

Toby seemed to realize they were all staring at him now, along with the coaches.

Joe Tyler said, "How come you never told me you could throw a football like that?"

Toby shrugged.

"You never asked me," he said.

CHAPTER

32

It had been an amazing day, Will thought when he was back in his room.

Like the season had been amazing from the start.

From the time he'd fumbled in last year's championship game, turning one of the best days of his life into one of the worst, he'd dreamed about the day when he'd play the Castle Rock Bears again with the whole season on the line.

Now that game was less than a week away.

But if somebody had told him how he'd get here, how they'd all get here—how his dad would get here and Toby's dad and even Hannah Grayson—Will Tyler would have thought somebody had made the whole thing up.

And on top of that, if somebody had also told Will they were going to try to beat the big, bad Bears of Castle Rock with just ten players, he would have had to borrow one of Tim's favorite words:

He would have thought they were *buggin'*.

But here they were.

A girl had joined the team and then Toby had, too. Tim had left. Chris had broken his ankle at the worst-possible time, not that there was ever a particularly special time for something like that to happen.

Will and his dad had done this together. Somehow Toby and *his* dad had done the same thing. Only now they had to find a way to finish the job, against the best and deepest team in the league.

But how?

Will sat on the windowsill for a while, staring out at Valley Road. No answers for him out there. No answer when he looked up at the stars in the sky. No answer when he stretched out on his bed and stared at the ceiling.

No way to make the sides even between now and Saturday.

He thought: *We need an eleventh man.*

The Bulldogs were so close to pushing the ball across the line, they just needed a little push, like the one Matt Leinart gave Reggie Bush in a famous USC–Notre Dame game that Will loved to watch on ESPN Classic.

One more time, Will knew he had to try something.

But what?

One more desperation heave, that's what.

One more Hail Mary.

He got up off the bed and opened his laptop and sent Hannah a Facebook message.

A few minutes later she sent back a message of her own.

Luv it. Go 4 it.

Then Will was all the way back to the beginning, to where this had all started for him and the Bulldogs and his dad and everybody else:

He wrote one more letter.

CHAPTER 33

The last practice before the championship game was Thursday night at Shea.

It was Toby's last chance to complete his crash course in being a quarterback, one more chance for all of them to become familiar with Mr. Keenan's crazy defenses.

But that wasn't what they were all talking about once they were together on the field. What they were all talking about was the latest edition of the Forbes *Dispatch*, which came out on Thursday afternoons.

They were talking about the story Hannah's dad had splashed across the front page.

One written "by Will Tyler."

Will had seen it as soon as he came home from school and had called Hannah right away.

"It was only supposed to be a letter to the editor," he said.

"And that's exactly what I told my dad," she had said. "But he thought it ought to be more." She giggled. "Besides, you know you can't trust the press."

The headline on the front page read:

A Team for Our Town

Then came Will's byline, and underneath that, the letter—what he *thought* was a letter—he had written on Monday night. Since Hannah's dad was the editor, Will had begun by writing "Dear Mr. Grayson."

Turned out to be the only thing Mr. Grayson had changed. Here was the rest of it:

> *I'm sure not everybody in town knows about it, but our twelve-year-old team, the Bulldogs, plays for the championship of the West River league this Saturday afternoon at Shea.*
>
> *We almost didn't have a team this season, because there wasn't enough money in the town council budget, which everybody knows by now. But then we got lucky and New Balance came through for us (big-time!) and sponsored our team. Now we get another shot at Castle Rock, which beat us in last year's championship game.*
>
> *The reason I am writing this letter is pretty much the same reason I wrote to Mr. Rob DeMartini of New Balance right before our season that almost wasn't:*

Because we need a little more help.

No, it's not money this time if that's what you think. We just need for people in our town to get behind us in a different way, which means by being our eleventh man on Saturday.

And that's not a mistake on my part. I know that usually in football, people talk about the crowd being the "twelfth man." Well, that doesn't apply in our case because we're down to ten players now.

It's why we hope Forbes can get behind us on Saturday, and maybe even Friday night, too.

My dad, Joe Tyler (he's also my coach), told me that when he used to play at Forbes High, there'd be pep rallies in the Square on Friday night. He said that it was almost like the game started right there and you could hear the cheers all over town.

My dad says that maybe one more time Forbes could cheer that way for one of its teams.

My dad also says that one of the best things about sports is when it makes us feel as if we're all in something together.

I guess that's what I'm asking for now. And promising that if you help make the sides even, me and my teammates won't let you down.

Sincerely,

Will Tyler,

Forbes Bulldogs

Joe Tyler had brought their copy of the paper with him to practice, even though Will had begged him not to. When they were all together on the field, the way they were before the start of every practice, he just held up the paper and said, "I don't have to say anything tonight because Will said it all."

Will knew he was blushing, could feel his face overheating, also knew there was nothing he could do about it except put on his helmet. That's when Hannah said, "Not only does he have the right stuff on the field, now we find out he's got the *w-r-i-t-e* stuff."

"Tell me you didn't just say that," Will said.

"I had to," she said.

"Hey, everybody listen up," Will's dad said now. "Before we get to work, I've really only got one announcement to make. I'd like everybody to show up at McElroy Square tomorrow night around seven o'clock. No pads or anything. Just your uniforms. Just one last chance for us to get together as a team before the big game. For a pizza party to end all pizza parties."

Chris Aiello was with them on the field, on crutches, his ankle in a soft cast.

"Look what you started," he said to Will.

Joe Tyler made a gesture that took in all of the Bulldogs, and then said to Will, "Yeah. Look what you started." It wasn't a pizza party.

And only the Bulldogs had been told to show up at seven o'clock. Everybody else in town had gotten the word—on the newspaper's website and on the local radio station—to be in McElroy Square by six thirty.

When Will and his dad pulled up next to the Flyers factory, Will couldn't believe his eyes.

The Square was already full of people.

"You were in on this," Will said to his dad.

"I was," Joe Tyler said. "But we can still go for pizza afterward if you want."

Will was still staring at the crowd.

"I didn't even know there *were* this many people left in Forbes," Will said.

"Maybe," his dad said, "there's still more life to this old town than we thought."

When his dad got out of the car, he was facing the factory. Then looking up and pointing. And smiling.

Will saw what his dad saw then, the huge banner stretched across the top two floors, saw lights shining in the windows up there, if only for this one night.

The banner read:

Go Bulldogs!

"Now it really does seem like old times," Joe Tyler said.

Across the street, at the head of the park near the old World War II monument, they saw where the temporary stage had been erected, a microphone at the front of it, a long row of chairs behind it.

As Will and his dad made their way into the park, they saw a man waving at them from the stage.

"Who's that?" Will said.

"*That,* pal, is Mr. Rob DeMartini of New Balance. He called and told me he was flying in this afternoon. Said he figured this was as good a time as any for the two of you to finally meet."

Will was surprised at how young Mr. DeMartini was, not looking much older than Joe Tyler. Dark hair and a nice smile.

"At last we meet," Mr. DeMartini said, shaking Will's hand.

"I can't believe you're here."

"No, actually, I can't believe *you're* here," Mr. DeMartini said.

"We didn't exactly make things easy on ourselves," Will said.

"Your dad's been keeping me up to speed every week," Mr. DeMartini said, "including what happened to Chris. No worries, that will just make beating Castle Rock even sweeter."

Now Mr. DeMartini pulled Will aside, so it was just the two of them.

"But whatever happens tomorrow," he said, "you kept your word, Will. You made all of us at New Balance proud."

Before long the rest of the Bulldogs had taken their places on the stage. When they were all there, the crowd cheered. But Will wasn't looking out into the crowd, he was looking at his dad, who was staring up at the banner again. And somehow in that moment Will could see the kid his dad had been once, understood what nights like this must have meant to him.

Mr. DeMartini stepped to the microphone now, introduced himself, explained how New Balance had come to sponsor the Bulldogs, then said, "This team is everything we want our company to stand for. We tell our people every day that we want them to be the best. And these kids behind me expect to be the best tomorrow against Castle Rock."

The crowd cheered again.

"Everybody in my business knows about the Forbes Flyers," he said, "and what they meant to this town once. Maybe that's why it's nice to see those lights back on across the street, even if it's only for one night."

Another cheer.

"And tomorrow afternoon," he said, "the Bulldogs are going to make Forbes feel like a winner again, and do the thing that sports still does best: make a memory."

Now the crowd made a sound that maybe only Will's dad, and Toby's dad, understood. Maybe because the people here sounded happy.

Then Will's dad was at the microphone, introducing the Bulldogs one by one.

He saved Will until last.

"Finally," he said, "I'd like to introduce my son, Will Tyler, with an old line of Yogi Berra's that kind of fits the occasion. From the bottom of my heart, I want to thank my son for making this night necessary."

He motioned Will up to the microphone then. Will shook his head. But then Hannah was pulling him out of his seat, saying, "You've so got this."

Will bought himself some time by adjusting the microphone, but then he decided he didn't need a speech, he was going to keep it simple:

"Beat Castle Rock," he said into the microphone.

He didn't yell, but the crowd did now, making a sound in McElroy Square that Will was sure they could hear on the other side of the river.

Will hoping in that moment that the Bulldogs hadn't heard anything yet.

34

When Will came downstairs, already in uniform, his dad was holding the New Balance box like it was an early Christmas present.

"Mr. DeMartini dropped this off while you were in the shower," Joe Tyler said.

Will took the box from him, opened it and smiled. New football shoes. Exactly like the ones he'd been wearing all season, except for one added feature:

The wings on the sides.

The New Balance version of the old Forbes Flyers.

"How . . . ?" Will said.

"Well," his dad said, "he might have had a *little* help with the design."

"It's like they're the last Forbes Flyers in existence," Will said.

"No," his dad said. "Actually, the last Forbes Flyer would be *you*."

Will put on the shoes. They felt as if he'd been wearing them all season.

He stood up. Time for them to go.

They walked out the front door and got into the car for the short ride to what Will, even at twelve, already knew was the best place in the world: the big game.

It was as if the crowd from the Square had come straight from there to Shea Field. By the time they were ten minutes away from the kick, the bleachers were full on the home side of Shea for the first time this season. Not only were the bleachers full, the Forbes fans were stretched out four and five deep from both ends.

The Castle Rock fans had to use the smaller bleachers on the other side.

Hannah said, "Must have been that long speech of yours last night that got people to come out."

"Funny."

She shrugged. "As always." Then she pointed to his new shoes. "Cool kicks," she said.

"You noticed."

"Hey," she said, "of course I noticed shoes, I'm a girl."

Kendrick had tried to start chirping early, while both teams were warming up. Edging as close to the Bulldogs as he possibly could without actually *joining* their warm-ups. When he was about ten yards away, he made a big show out of counting the players.

"Wait," he said. "You must be one short. No matter how many times I count, I still only come up with ten little Indians."

Will tried to ignore him. They all did. Except for Toby, the one who usually had the least to say. Will hadn't heard him say a word to an opposing player all season, the only exception being with Kendrick, when he'd run him off behind the bleachers.

But Toby made one more exception now, walking slowly toward where Kendrick was doing all his talking. Will moved up a little closer so he could hear.

"Try to learn something new every day," Toby said, big grin on the big guy's face. "Now I already have today."

Will watched Kendrick as Toby got close to him, saw the swagger falling off him like sweat.

"What's that you learned?"

"That you can count, Kendrick," he said.

Kendrick's comeback was so weak Will wondered why he'd even bothered.

"Well," he said, "we'll see who's talking at the end of the game."

Toby said, "Oh, I expect you'll be. But what you'll be talking about is us holding up the trophy."

Toby turned and jogged toward the sideline with the rest of the Bulldogs, over to where Will's dad and Toby's dad were waiting for them in front of their bench.

"The time for talking is over," Joe Tyler said. "You deserve to be here today. I believe you were *meant* to be here today. The only thing left for you to do now is play a game that you're going to remember for the rest of your lives."

He put his hand out. They put their hands on top of his.

"Don't make me proud today, or all those people in the stands," Will's dad said. "Make yourselves proud."

He looked at each face, one by one, finally stopping at Will's.

"I'd give my *good* knee to have one more game like this to play."

He came into the season saying he wasn't a shouter. Didn't shout now. Kept his voice low.

"Bulldogs," he said.

"Bulldogs," they said back to him.

Joe Tyler was right. Time for talking was over. Time to play Castle Rock.

A couple of times during warm-ups Ben Clark had tried to get Will's attention, but Will had ignored him. They could go back to being friends when the game was over.

All season long, Joe Tyler had picked a different captain for every game. But today, all of the Bulldogs went out for the coin toss.

All ten of them.

"Safety in numbers?" Hannah said to Will.

"That only works," Will said to her, "if you actually *have* the numbers."

They won the toss, elected to receive. Kendrick looked like he wanted to say something, but the ref was standing right there.

So was Toby.

Will ran down to his position, waited for Ben Clark's kick.

It was a surprisingly short one, considering the leg Ben had. Will's dad would tell him later he caught it, in full stride, at the Bulldogs' thirty-yard line.

He took it straight up the middle, not worrying that he had one less blocker than usual, just looking for a seam. Saw one open to his right, Toby's side, got to it before it closed.

Cut to the right sideline.

And just like that, like it was too good to be true, Will was in the clear, all this green grass in front of him, running free, running one more time like he had Shea Field to himself.

He just looked over his shoulder one time, to see where the defense was, saw Kendrick angling across the field at full speed but knowing that as fast as Kendrick was, he had no chance.

None.

The only trash talk right now was inside Will's head.

Eat my dust.

He was still ten yards ahead of Kendrick when he crossed the goal line, handed the ball to the ref, waited for his teammates at this end of the field, high-fived them when they got to him, made sure not to look like he'd lost his mind over the first play of the game, even one like this.

The crowd on the Forbes side of the field, however, was going nuts. Will had never heard such thunder at Shea.

Hannah kicked the point. Just like that it was 7–0. Before the Bulldogs kicked off, Dick Keenan yelled for them to come over to where he was standing.

"Okay, boys and girls," he said. "Now comes the hard part: trying to trick them into thinking we're the ones have *them* outnumbered."

Somehow they kept the Bears scoreless in the first quarter. Toby sacked Ben three times and forced Kendrick to fumble. Mr. Keenan made sure the Bulldogs never gave Ben the same look on defense, never used the same blitz twice in the same series of downs. He kept calling out the coverages and formations to Toby, sometimes just using hand signals. Toby would nod and then tell his teammates what they were doing, totally in command, Toby and his dad connected on this day every bit as much as Will and Joe Tyler were.

The Bulldogs stretched their lead early in the second quarter. Toby, who had to be stronger than any quarterback Castle Rock had seen this season, got away from one of their blitzes, shrugging off their middle linebacker like he wasn't even there. He scrambled to his right and threw the ball as far as he could to Will, who'd gotten behind the Bears' free safety, Will running under the ball at the Bears' five-yard line before scoring, the ball having traveled fifty-five yards in the air.

Like Toby was born to throw a football this way. Same as he was born to be this kind of football player.

The Bears blocked Hannah's extra-point attempt, flooding one side of the line, so many guys smothering the ball Will wasn't even sure which one got it.

It was still 13–0, Bulldogs. Somehow the game Will had

dreamed this long about playing had turned *into* a dream game. For now.

On his way back up the field, Will ran past Chris Aiello, who tossed him a water bottle. Chris still had his crutches but was moving up and down the sidelines like a champ.

"How we lookin'?" Chris said.

"Long way to go," Will said. "They're too good not to figure it out eventually."

"Yeah," Chris said, "but they're getting frustrated. Like they can't believe this is happening to them."

"Neither can I," Will said.

It was here that the Bears *did* begin to figure it out. Instead of having Ben Clark try to out-guess Mr. Keenan's crazy defenses, try to find the open man that had to be out there somewhere against ten-man defenses, the Bears decided to just pound the ball instead, running the ball on just about every play of the ensuing drive, sometimes right at Toby, almost like they were trying to use his speed against him, his ability to pursue to catch him out of position.

To Will, the drive seemed to take forever. Mr. Keenan didn't just give in to them, he kept trying to trick things up, but right now tricks had no chance against old-fashioned, smashmouth football.

All of a sudden, it was as if the Bears *did* have the numbers on them. They threw the ball only twice on the drive, both short passes to Kendrick. The other eleven plays were running plays, the last a quarterback sneak from Ben for a touchdown. On their two-point conversion attempt it looked as if Ben planned to keep the ball on an option play, but right before Toby just planted him to the turf, Ben pitched the ball to Kendrick and it was 13–8.

Still 13–8 at the half.

Will wanted to feel happy about their five-point lead. Wanted to be happy that they had *any* kind of lead. But he wasn't. He understood the game he was watching, could already see the defense starting to tire, especially the guys up front, on what was way too hot a day for the first week of November in Forbes.

Joe Tyler obviously saw it, too, in the players who'd flopped into the grass behind the bench first chance they got.

"Everybody up," he said. "Right now."

The Bulldogs got to their feet.

"And when we go out there to kick," he said, "I don't want you walking out. Or jogging out there. I want everybody on this team to *sprint*. Then I want you to start pounding on each other the way guys in the pros and college do in the tunnel *before* the game. Like this game is just starting. Got it?"

They all nodded.

"I know you guys get tired of some of my quotes sometimes," he said. "But my last one for this season is one that applies pretty good here: fatigue makes cowards out of us all. Only it's not going to make cowards out of *us*. Because this is the toughest football team I've ever been around."

He looked at Will now. "You got anything?"

Will did, actually.

"It's like the coach says at the end of *Miracle*," he said, refer-ring to his all-time favorite sports movie, the one about the Lake Placid Olympic hockey team that beat the Russians in the Olym-pics. "Their time is over," Will said, pointing over at the Bears, smiling as he did. "It's done. This is our time."

The Bulldogs started barking then, like they'd all gone whacked-out crazy at once.

But then, Will thought, *maybe this whole thing has been crazy from the start.*

Ben Clark came out in the second half acting like one of those cool quarterbacks in the pros, not deciding on the play until he got to the line of scrimmage and saw where Toby was lined up. Like Ben was waiting out Toby, and his dad. Will knew he had the smarts to do it, having grown up playing against him in all sports. Now the Castle Rock coach, Mr. Lyman, was putting the game in his hands, like Ben was Peyton Manning, his coach trusting him enough to change the play he'd called in the huddle anytime he wanted to.

Like a twelve-year-old quarterback wasn't just trying to out-wait Toby, he was trying to out-guess Toby's dad.

And succeeding at it right now, more often than not.

It had gotten Dick Keenan to start yelling at Toby again, like he was back up in the top row of the stands.

"Come *on*," he said, after the Bears lined up in a passing formation and then ran a draw play right past Toby. "This kid is kicking your tail!"

Will was playing corner on the side of Shea closest to the Bulldogs' bench. And couldn't help himself. Didn't want this to start up again now, because they had all come too far, Dick Keenan included.

"He's kicking *our* tails, Mr. Keenan," Will said. "*All* of ours."

He saw Mr. Keenan's face get redder than it already was, saw him take in a big gulp of air, like he was fighting for control.

He won the fight this time.

Maybe because he knew that *he'd* come too far.

"You're right, kid," he said finally. "The one gettin' bounced around right now is me."

No matter what defense he tried, though, the Bears were moving the ball now, Ben mixing passes with runs, picking on Hannah with most of the passes. Johnny tried to cheat to her side of the field from where he was playing safety, especially when Kendrick was over there. Even double-teamed, Kendrick was too big and too good for both of them.

They finally had first-and-goal at the eight. Ben went with a quick count, stepped up, threw to Kendrick in the flat. He caught the ball, ran over Hannah at the five, went in untouched from there.

Ben went right back to Kendrick for the two-point conversion, a perfectly thrown jump ball lob pass.

Now it was 16–13, Bears.

And Hannah was hurt.

Will could see it in the way she was moving even as she tried not to let on. Before he went back to return the kick, he got alongside her and said, "You okay?"

"Fine," she said.

"Liar."

She said, "That's my line, you dope."

They were close enough that Will could see her eyes, so red he wondered if she'd been crying.

Before he could say anything more, she said, "I'm not coming out."

Will grinned. "Wouldn't let you even if you wanted to," he said. "I was just gonna tell you to rub some dirt on it and walk it off."

He shrugged and said, "It's, like, a guy thing to say."

"Wow," Hannah said. "Don't guys ever run out of deep things like that to say?"

The Bulldogs, getting more tired by the minute, managed to get to midfield on their next series, mostly on Will's running. Yet they got stopped on downs and had to punt.

The Bears started to move the ball again, but Kendrick took his eyes off the ball when he was running free over the middle of the field and dropped the pass, and then Toby made a huge third-down sack on Ben.

The Bears punted. One minute into the fourth quarter, the Bulldogs had the ball back at their own forty-two-yard line. Will thinking: *Biggest game I've ever played.* Biggest crowd he'd ever seen at Shea, still applauding, as if sensing their team needed their energy.

Mr. DeMartini had come out of the stands and was standing with Will's dad and Mr. Keenan. He too was cheering on the Bulldogs.

Before the team went back on the field, Joe Tyler put his hands on his son's pads, put his face as close as it could get to his face mask.

"Take us home, kid," he said.

"Take a look around, Dad," Will said. "We *are* home."

Toby hit Johnny for a first down. A bullet to the sideline. Then a handoff to Will went for eight more. They were at the Bears' forty now. Second and two, Will feeling that the team had one more drive in them.

They ran one of their go-to plays, 37 Sweep to the left. Will waited for his blocking, the way he always did, knew he had the first down easily.

Until somebody punched the ball out of his hands.

It went flying through the air as if Will had pitched it ahead.

For a second, Will thought—*prayed*—it would roll out-of-bounds before anybody on the Bears could fall on it.

But it died, came to a dead stop, about a yard short of the sideline.

Sitting there, in Will's mind, for about six lifetimes.

"Ball!" somebody yelled.

Then he saw Kendrick closing on it from the secondary and Will knew, just knew, that Kendrick wasn't looking to just fall on the ball, he was looking to pick it up and run down the sideline with the score that could put the game out of reach for the Bulldogs.

But as he leaned down, suddenly Hannah Grayson appeared out of nowhere, launching herself at the ball, sliding in front of Kendrick and underneath him at the same time like a soccer goalie making a diving save, pushing the ball out-of-bounds.

Because it had been the Bulldogs' ball when it went out-of-bounds, it was still their possession.

This time Will's fumble hadn't cost his team the big game.

He started breathing again. The entire crowd seemed to exhale as one.

In the huddle, Hannah poked him with an elbow.

"You're welcome," she said.

Four plays later, though, the offense stalled. The Bulldogs had moved the ball down to the Bears' six, but then an offsides penalty against Wes on second-and-goal moved them back five yards. Will then got stopped for no gain, a great play by Ben Clark fighting off two blockers. Third-and-goal from the eleven. Toby wanted to throw it to Will in the flat, but the Bears came with a blitz and Toby was lucky to get back to the line of scrimmage.

Fourth-and-goal from the eleven.

They could go for it. Or they could try a field goal, from twenty-eight yards away.

Joe Tyler called them over and said, "We tie it here and take our chances in regulation, or overtime."

Will said, "I'm good with that." Looked at Hannah. "You good with that?"

"Pretty much my whole life," she said.

The Bears tried to load up the left side again to block the kick, but Toby switched over there right before the snap. The move was money, same as the snap and the hold.

The kick? Center cut.

Bulldogs 16, Bears 16.

Hannah said to Will, and only to Will, "You don't have to say it. But now you *really* like me."

Four minutes left at Shea, the Bulldogs hoping for one more chance on offense.

Only they could not stop the Castle Rock Bears now. The crowd was doing its best to be the eleventh man he'd asked them to be, the people even louder than they'd been all game long, stamping their feet on the old bleachers, even doing the wave a few times.

Then they started chanting "Bull-DOGS!" all over again.

But this *was* Will's nightmare, what had been his real nightmare all along, the one where his teammates were gassed at the end, too tired to win the game, heart having only taken them so far. It didn't even help that the Bears had to start their last drive at their own fifteen after an illegal-block-to-the-back penalty on the kickoff. Didn't help, didn't matter.

Even deep in his own territory, Ben went to work. Like this was his moment, not Will's.

He was finding the open man now, whether it was his tight end or one of the other wide receivers, usually Kendrick. When they ran the ball, it was for six, or eight, or ten yards.

Bears at midfield, in what felt like a blink. Ben kept it on the option. Ten yards to the Bulldogs' forty. Two minutes left. Ben threw one to Kendrick over the middle for twelve more yards.

Will's dad called his second time-out to give his guys a breather.

The Bears came out of it and Ben hit his tight end again. Ball on the twenty now. Ben taking all the time in the world between plays, purposely running down the clock as he dissected the Bulldogs' defense. He ran the option again, but Toby saw this one coming and stopped Ben for no gain.

Joe Tyler called his last time-out.

Thirty seconds left.

Second-and-ten, Bears.

Now Mr. Lyman, the Bears' coach, called time-out.

In the huddle, Will said to Toby, "You want to know why you came back?"

"For a game like this?"

"No," Will said, "you came back to get in Ben Clark's face on this play."

On the way out of the huddle Will grabbed Johnny Callahan and told him how the game was supposed to end.

For both teams.

Kendrick lined up on the right but then went in motion toward the other side of Shea. So that Hannah would have to cover him one more time.

Ben was in the shotgun, not even waiting to see where Toby lined up this time. Almost like he didn't care. Like the ending was inevitable, the Castle Rock Bears winning this kind of game because they always did.

Toby lined up outside the defensive end but then curled back to the middle as the ball was snapped, threw the Bears' center out of the way, came straight for Ben like a truck at full throttle.

Kendrick put a filthy head fake on Hannah, broke it to the outside. Beat her easily. Headed for the corner of the end zone, his favorite place in the world.

Running free again.

Ben had to rush the throw slightly because Toby *was* in his face. Because of one last Dick Keenan blitz. No matter. Ben still had time to let it go. Knowing he just had to get it anywhere near Kendrick, as wide open as he was.

Only he wasn't wide open.

Not anymore.

Because it wasn't Johnny playing safety now, it was Will Tyler. Because Will had switched with Johnny coming out of the huddle. Because he was *sure* the ball was going to Kendrick, sure he had to catch the game-winning pass, and so he had read the play all the way.

Will came flying from the middle of the field, cut in front of Kendrick Morris, didn't even have to jump.

Picked off the ball clean.

Behind him Will heard Kendrick scream, *"Nooooo!"*

Oh yes, Will thought.

Yes.

He was already at top speed coming out of the end zone, coming fast, as fast as the play had turned around. The Forbes Flyer. Shea opening up for him now like his front door. Running past his dad, who was hobbling down the sideline, waving him on. Running past Dick Keenan, past Mr. DeMartini of New Balance.

Saw that the last kid from Castle Rock with a chance at him was Ben Clark. Ben had a pretty decent angle on him, running as hard as he could.

Will waited until Ben was a step away.

Then he made his cut.

On the fly.

One of those high-speed cuts his dad said you had to be born being able to make. Cut to his left without breaking stride and fooled Ben Clark so badly he went down, like he'd been dropped by a punch.

Then there was nothing in front of Will Tyler except the end zone, and the touchdown that made it 22–16 and won the championship for the Bulldogs.

35

When it was officially over, after the Bulldogs knocked down one last desperation pass from Ben Clark to Kendrick as the game clock expired, the Bulldogs picked up Will and carried him around the field until he yelled at them to put him down.

Mr. Keenan got both Will and Toby into a bear hug then and said, "Told you two showboats that defense wins."

Will made his way to midfield, because that's where Hannah Grayson was. He had tossed his helmet toward the Bulldogs' bench by then. She had done the same. Just the two of them, in the middle of all the craziness going on around them at Shea. For once, she didn't say anything smart, didn't say anything at all, just leaned over and kissed him on the cheek and nearly dropped him easier than the Bears ever had.

They had the trophy presentation a few minutes later, and what felt like the whole town of Forbes cheered again. When it was over, Joe Tyler handed his cell phone to Will, and the next thing he heard was a lot of yelling from Tim LeBlanc in Scottsdale, Arizona.

It wasn't until Will and his dad were home, just the two of them, door closed, that Joe Tyler told him that the athletics director from Forbes High School, Mr. Novak, had grabbed him after the game and asked if he might be interested in coaching his old school now that Coach Carson was retiring.

Will said, "What did you tell him?"

His dad grinned and said, "I told him I'd be very interested, as long as I could bring my mean old defensive coordinator along with me."

Joe Tyler hugged his son now, as hard as he ever had. When he pulled back, he said, "It's like I always told you: I could run. Just not like you."

"We made this run together, Dad. You and me. We did it together."

The pizza party at Vicolo's was scheduled for seven thirty. It gave Will and Hannah plenty of time to meet at his favorite rock overlooking the river.

To sit there with the silver championship trophy between them.

"You knew he'd throw it to Kendrick," she said.

"Had to."

"Because I was covering him?"

"Wouldn't have mattered if Toby had been covering him, along with a couple of Steelers," Will said. "Kendrick had to be the hero. It had to go to him."

She gave him one more smile now. Put her hand in his as if that were the most natural thing in the world for her to do.

And maybe it was one of the lights from one of the boats in the river then, reflecting off the trophy. Or an early star in the sky. Or Hannah's smile. Maybe that was it. But in that moment it was as if somebody had just thrown a spotlight on where they were sitting.

And Will wondered what they were thinking in Castle Rock right now, wondered if somebody over there was wondering where the light was coming from on the Forbes side of the river.

"You're wrong," Hannah said. "You had to be the hero. The ball had to go to you."

"I didn't drop it this time," Will said.